East of Coker

East
of
Coker

Andy Owen

Published by The War Writers' Campaign, Inc.
PO Box 3811
Parker, Colorado

ISBN: 978-0692653890

Library of Congress Control Number: 2016934604

Photo/cover/credits: AJ van der Westhuyzen

Disclaimer: The Publisher and the Author make no representations or warranties with respect to the accuracy or completeness of the contents of this work and specifically disclaim all warranties, including without limitation warranties of fitness for a particular purpose. No warranty may be created or extended by sales or promotional materials. The advice and strategies contained herein may not be suitable for every situation. This work is sold with the understanding that neither the Publisher nor the Author shall be liable for damages arising therefrom. The fact that an organization or website is referred to, does not mean that the Publisher endorses any information that said organization or website may provide, or recommendations it may make. Further, readers should be aware that Internet websites listed in this work might have changed or disappeared between when this work was written and when it is read.

All proceeds of this literary work go to The War Writers' Campaign, Inc. and/or any charitable cause The War Writers' Campaign, Inc. deems to distribute.

Dedication

'For Katie, Max and Lawrence'

East of Coker

'For once I saw with my own eyes the Cumean Sibyl hanging in a jar, and when the boys asked her, "Sibyl, what do you want?" she answered, "I want to die."'

-Petronius Arbiter, Satyricon

I cannot remember what it is like to not be in pain. It is having to perform for the parade of victim hunters that gets me more than the pain or the boredom. The presenters and their bone questions and the accompanying crew who treat us like a prop or at best one of those fame-hungry idiots on your shit TV, no-talent shows – as if we have asked for the chance to be part of whatever it is they are doing. As if we want to be here. Avoiding swearing is tiring. The charity workers turning up with their oversized cheques for their photo opportunity who, although mean well, are almost as bad. You want to see we are alright, so you don't have to feel bad about forgetting we are still here, or what's left of us anyway – we are all missing something here; hands, feet, arms, legs, sight or something worse. There are lots of spare trainers and gloves here, and not just the individual, unused ones from pairs where only one is required, but complete pairs too: socks given to those with no legs, and gloves to those with no hands. For birthdays and other landmarks, as jokes that never get old. It is how we cope. For me, now I am off the morphine, it is the drink that helps me cope as much as the jokes.

We too are culpable though. We play a role: the role of the plucky soldier, who will crack on anyway in good humour, despite our physical incapacity. When the camera or Dictaphone is pointed at us, we won't complain. We will just crack on, taking the piss out of ourselves and each other as we do; 'You have lost weight' is the standard greeting those who have lost a limb get when seeing mates they have not seen since. More recently, those now coming in from Afghanistan have lost quite a bit of weight as the Taliban move to greater use of IEDs and we get better at keeping people alive. I never got as far as Afghanistan; my injuries were from Iraq.

We will learn to walk again, to talk again, to do things we used to take for granted. Things we can never take for granted again. When pushed on how we feel about others who didn't make it, there will be a pause, a look away and then a look back with a new, more determined glare. We have those old men from previous wars who stand tall and silent at the Remembrance Day parades we have attended as our role models. We aspire to their stoic pride. Some here will never get better from their injuries; legs don't tend to grow back. Some may never get back to where we want to be; there are many here, mostly the younger blokes, who think they will one day re-join their units again. I know I will never serve again with The Corps, and that will leave a hole bigger than any bit of shrapnel has left.

Marcus, one of the young officers (who actually seems alright – I have had some I would not follow even out of curiosity and one or two that would have been out of their depth in a puddle), was telling us some Greek myth about some bloke who had to push the rock up the mountain only for it to roll back down again as soon as he reached the summit. It is not ideal, but what else are you going to do? You have got to keep pushing the rock even if you know on some level that it will only roll back down again. Got to keep fighting regardless; giving up is not an option. It then becomes about the fight itself and the defiance of fighting on, despite the odds, despite knowing ultimately how fruitless the fight will be.

I am starting to realise, though, that it is the wounds you cannot see that incapacitate more than those that you can see. I am not talking about the neuro wing that deals with those with physical brain injuries, although we feel for them the most. Even the 'bilats' – those who have lost both legs above the knee – wouldn't swap places with them. They are the ones that leave no physical mark. The ones you don't ask about on your brief visits. Those are the ones we don't talk about, when those professionals who weren't over there, but whose job it is to ask try to engage us, try to get us to talk or get us to "think of waterfalls". Those are the ones I won't talk about with anyone. Instead, I drink so I don't have to think about them when I am alone. I am constantly asked about my hopes for the future, yet I cannot turn my head round from looking at the past. The expectation is that I will have plans of Paralympic glory, or of an extreme fundraising expedition to one of the poles, or scaling several peaks. Sometimes all I want to tell them is that I wish I had been left to die; left to sink into the murky river that I had been thrown into by the blast. Sometimes I want to die.

'One generation passeth away, and another generation cometh; but the earth abideth forever... The sun also ariseth, and the sun goes down, and hasteth to the place where he rose... The wind goeth toward the south, and turneth about unto the north; it whirleth about continually, and the wind returneth again according to his circuits... All rivers run into the sea; yet the sea is not full; unto the place from whence the rivers come, thither they return again'.

-Ecclesiastes

I: The Burial of the Dead—South East London—Spring 2011

April is the cruellest month. As the dull roots are bathed with April showers, so I want to bathe every vein in different liquor, to remain numb, to avoid stirring memories buried under the snow of time. As the world wakes from winter and rejuvenation is the theme, I am reminded of what I lost, what is still missing, what is no longer a part of me. I sit on the cold bench, old dry bones aching in the leaching sunlight. I see the children playing soldiers, laughing as they mimic the noises that still echo through my mind in the quiet times. They are mostly quiet times these days, as the memories of the music we used to dance to fade away. I fold the corner of the page after reading, 'Society is a partnership between those who are living, those who are dead, and those who are yet to be born', and gently close the battered book. I have nothing invested in those who are not yet born. I see no ties with the world that happens after my life ends, after what makes this conscious me 'me' is annihilated. In my end, there are no beginnings. There is nothing left for me to invest in now in the hope that it continues post my mortem. Not only because I have no children I want to watch grow, no genes to see carried on, but the values I have tried to live my life by have also died. I have nothing invested in the future after my passing that gives my present meaning. I survive now only so they, the fallen, survive; as when I die, all memory of them as people dies forever. The expressions never caught on camera, but glimpsed; the thoughts never written down, but shared in conversation; the majority of interactions that we have that are only left behind in the minds of others, will all be gone. Their memories have already been stolen and used to send others to their deaths, by people who did not know them, but are happy to speak for them. Happy to say, 'This is what they were fighting for, this is what they believed'. Others will be offered immortality through dying to preserve those beliefs, but they are not the same beliefs as we held back then.

I feel like people can tell and see me as a burden. I am one of those old male deer, their rutting days behind them, shunned from the rest of the herd and forced to wander alone. I can only look back to what I owe those who are now dead, and no-one wants to hear what that form of nostalgia is really like. I often think about how the men I killed were once small children. Killing someone tends, in my experience, to split people into two camps – in one camp, you have those who develop a profound respect for life. I am in this camp. In the other camp, you have those who quickly become immune or desensitised; some in this camp may even enjoy the killing, becoming defined by their ability to inflict violence. I feared killing as much as I feared being killed, perhaps even more. I developed such a respect for life that I have dedicated all these years to trying to keep those alive who are already dead. If only we had all seen how we were as children back then, maybe we would not have been able to do what we did to each other. How did I do what I did? But we were men, and we looked like men back then, not like the adult-children of today, still dressing like teenagers when they have teenagers themselves. It is less tragic for men to die than boys. Regardless of what a boy may grow to be, for him to die before he is allowed to become whatever he could become, is more tragic. We do not want to see pictures or hear stories of children dying. We say it is out of respect for them, but it is really because it is too sad to bear. A dead child misses out on losing his innocence, miss out on learning the world is not what he was brought up to believe. He misses out on finding out that not everything will be alright. He misses out on then working out how he will cope with that. He does not get to live the full story of his life, and that I find to be the saddest. As I sit here in the park, I hear distant thunder, which sounds like the echo of artillery, finally reaching back to me after all these years, having bounced off some celestial body. It is a sound I never got used to hearing. It is time to go. It is time for me to get moving again. I brush off the dust that accumulates on me whenever I sit still, and prepare to use my tired old legs.

I no longer remember what I looked like as a young child. No photographs have been passed down to me. There must have been many, but they have got lost between deaths and divorces. I am not sure I even believe I ever was a baby. I have no memories from before I must have been about five years old. I just have the remembered words of others and a belief in the unseen forces of causality: yet my memories are unreliable and science so confusing that I have come to doubt both. From when my memories start in the first person, I know nothing mattered to me back then; I had no cares that a kind word or a new day would not remedy. I would welcome the first sunshine of the spring, which seemed to closely follow Christmas, and herald the start of a new summer that would stretch away beyond my perceptible horizon. Every sunny afternoon felt like it would last forever. They did not though, and youth eventually ended. It is too late when you realise that it does matter how you spend the time you have. My mother would look at me with an affection her mother would once have looked upon her with and so on back to Eve. I am the end of that cycle, the break in the chain. Though not completely; my body when I am dead will be sown as seed in the soil of the land of my birth and fertilise new, unrelated life. I move past the children playing on swings, their light laughter carrying on the breeze. When I fell from the rope swing in our yard, I would call for my mother, who was then a young woman still, with hopes and dreams that I never knew. Some of the soldiers I saw being killed called for their mothers again at that final moment. I answered one such call. I whispered that it would all be okay when we both knew that it would not. No-one will call my name. I think I would have called your name too. I try not to think of those big words, which make us so unhappy. I am so numb that nothing matters now, but not in the same way that I remember as a boy.

The breeze is coming in over the snot-green sea to the south, blowing away the winter's detritus, like nature's broom. Even though it is spring now and we are meant to be coming out of the worst weather, it is one of those days when no matter which way you turn, it seems like the wind is blowing from that direction. Winter had kept us warm, covering Earth in forgetful snow. Past the playground, I stop at the Colonnade Cafe and find a table outside. Not the one I usually sit at, that is taken, but close enough to do. I move in small leaps and bounds now as if I was still avoiding being fixed by unseen enemy fire. I drink tea, write another letter, make an entry in my diary, and spend an hour reading the free papers, rather than the book in my pocket. History repeating endlessly: great cogs continuing to turn even though their creator is no longer present to watch their cycles. There is nothing new under the sun. I read stories about people I am meant to have heard of, behaving in ways that upset and bewilder me. The people passing me on the street speak a variety of different languages, none of which I understand. The waitress is foreign, and I cannot understand what she is asking me either, although I am sure that it is an English of sorts she is speaking. I am British – but what does that mean now? I don't recognise the country I grew up in or the community I was once part of. The tie holding the reptilian folds of my neck feels tight as I swallow my weak sweet tea, choking me, reminding me I am still alive, for now.

As I finish my tea and think of moving again, a woman of a

certain age – who must have no interesting business of her own, so feels obliged to interfere in the business of others – looks to engage me with sympathetic eyes, but I quickly turn away. I do not need her sympathy. She is the sort that if you see two people talking and one looks bored, she's the other one. She is from a generation which has failed to pass on to the next the values and sense of duty of those who died for them. Her generation will instead ask its children, who will always remain children, to work past the age they did, but without the comfort of their beliefs or any sort of community. Leaving them so scared to offend, they will allow the fascism we fought against to rise again in another form. They have bankrupted us financially and morally. They are Dante's Uncommitted, and will as such remain on the shores of the Acheron with the souls of people who in life did nothing, neither for good nor evil, neither in hell nor out of it. We are told their punishment will be to eternally pursue their own self-interest while being chased by wasps and hornets that will continually sting them. I roll a cigarette to ensure the woman does not approach. I take my lighter, which you gave me the day before I left all those years ago, from my jacket pocket and run my finger over where the inscription used to be before it was worn away by time.

> 'As easy might I from myself depart,
>   As from my soul, which in thy breast doth
>   Lie'.

When I look around now, what are the roots that clutch, what branches grow out of this stony rubbish, which is picked at by the pigeons? 'As we grow older the world becomes stranger, the pattern more complicated, of dead and living'. When it was announced that; 'God is dead', it was announced with concern, not with glee. There were concerns as to whether the science, the culture and the art of the time would fill the resulting moral vacuum. There were concerns as to whether there would be anything to fulfil our basic human need to have something to believe in, something which gives our lives meaning, something previously fulfilled through religion. This was at the time of the Weimar, where a culture based on the words of Goethe and Schiller blossomed to the music of Beethoven and Wagner, rather than the tell-tale diaries of the celebrities famous for being famous and the orange-faced warblers of today's no-talent shows. For many of us, God died in the trenches of two great wars, where His silence was more deafening than any enemy shelling. When, however, culture becomes as moribund as it is today, and, science and art so disconnected from how we live, God returns to fill the void. And He has returned, driving people to new trenches under black banners proclaiming his greatness. I have begun to think that all of humanity's most evil deeds have come when we have put ideals before people and, all our greatest deeds, when we have put people before ideals. This may say more about the quality of our ideals than I intended.

I did not fight for a God or any other transcendent belief before; as all soldiers from all sides ultimately do, I ended up fighting for my own survival, for the survival of the men next to me and for the survival of those back home – the people, not the nation. We did it because it was the right thing to do. We had confidence back then in what that meant. We were scared and sometimes were not as brave as people give us credit for now, but that is because we were human. After what I saw during the war, it was hard to ever consider a benevolent, omnipotent God, who would allow the suffering that I witnessed. It has been hard ever since to be confident what the right thing to do is. I think when I joined up, as I volunteered rather than being conscripted, I joined up to fight for the rights of people to be free from the worst of our humanity, not a set of rights that today's generation believe they are entitled to at birth, that provide a level of comfort and individualism that previous generations could not dream of. The right to be free from persecution, from tyranny and from harm, not the right to take a wage from the state just for existing, the right to own the latest television set or the freedom to behave as you please and not take any responsibility for your actions. 'Freedoms from' have become 'freedoms and rights to'. 'To be happy is not the purpose of our being; rather it is to deserve happiness'. I wrote that down in my diary, the first year I started to keep one, with the same pen I have used to write today's letter and diary entry. I know I am old fashioned. I am out of touch – one look at me will tell you this. That is part of the reason I have been cast out from the herd. Some would probably accuse me of being a fascist, even though I fought against them and they have not. At least I would be accused of being an old conservative, as an insult rather than a statement of fact, whose time has gone and who has nothing to teach to those coming next. Some no doubt would suspect that deep down, I am motivated by a hatred of those who are different, rather than a pride and respect for my own culture and traditions that evolved over hundreds of years through the input of many great men and women. Maybe for some this is true, but not for all. The fear of giving time to those for which it is true stifles the debate, and means that to many, I should not have a say anymore.

I know more than most that deep down we are all more alike than different. I have seen first-hand the one thing that unites us all. It is that we will all die. Like Koheleth, I know that the lives of the wise and foolish, rich and poor all end the same. I understand that all our superficial differences are a response to this universal fact: necessary illusions that help us hide from the fact that we know this is it and there is nothing else. So much of our culture and our notions of self are to buffer us against this fundamental fear of non-existence. These fragments we shore against our ruins. This is what I know anyway; deep in my core, even when singing in church as a boy, right from my beginning, I have been aware of the nature of my end. Anyway, there is no-one to make these accusations to me. These being-less voices of my imagination speak to me more than people in the world. Without the voices of others, I feel my being is fading away; it might as well be my end.

When I was a child staying at my cousin's in the lakes, he took me out on a sled, and I remember being frightened for the first time. I would be with my sister, we would hug, but now she is no more, and there is nothing of her left to touch. She is the only person I knew that well as a child and then saw get old and die, making her death all the worse. When she died, that little girl I loved died too. The fear was different then on that sled from the fear I felt later in war and the fear I have now. My cousin said, 'hold on tight', which is what I told myself as I heard the crack and the thump years later, and I tell myself still now every time I hear a door slam. And down we went and down I go. With no-one to listen, I can let my thoughts run free. I do not need to be constricted by the rules of conversation, or sense or order. In the mountains, you feel free, further from the earth's core; the air is lighter, and the sense you could just float away into the nothingness is stronger. I read much of the night then and I still read now, but my night is shorter, and more regularly interrupted. Sometimes on the way back to my bed, I turn off all the lights and move slowly in the dark by memory and touch. I stop in the middle of the room and listen in the darkness as if I am back in the jungle on sentry, listening for unseen others inching closer, senses heightened. In that darkness where I could not see my hand in front of my face, I felt more a part of the world than at any other time, my unseen body no longer separating me from everything else. 'This is the present', I used to say to myself in the dark. I was empty of everything, ready to react to whatever was yet unseen. After a while, before my eyes in the dark, I would start to see a brown background with turquoise, blue and green flashes, with flecks of orange-yellow, as well as geometrical patterns pulsating as my brain started to create its own stimuli. Since then, memories and expectations have seemed more real than the actual experiences in my present, even though the memories sometimes seem like they happened to someone else. Standing in my bedroom at night, I can now never empty myself of all that has filled me over the years. I have so few expectations, not believing my reward will come when my flesh is no more, and my memories are deserting me, but I can never fully bring myself to the present. Now is numbness.

I now go south in the winter as the nights get longer, to the edge of the land and the smell of the salt air, as many my age do. We congregate on deck chairs facing south, as if we are waiting for Charon, who will take us to the undiscovered country, to emerge from the sea as if it is the Styx. Each year, though, as winter ends and no sails are sighted, we greet this with a cheer rather than a sense of loss. What will He say to me when it is my turn; will He tell me it will be like those nights in the jungle when I felt at one with the world? My fate must be worse than that; I don't believe forgiveness can come so easily for what I have done; but as I have said, I am unsure there will be anyone to offer this forgiveness anyway. My arthritic, nicotine-stained fingers fumble in my long pockets for change, not for the boatman, but for the waitress who I cannot understand.

I think back not to the dusty south London office that took thirty years of my life. The hours of routine laid down so few memories, as only a small shaft of particles would be illuminated by the touch of the low autumn sun on those long afternoons, the rest left floating unseen in the stale air of the high ceilinged office. I think back to that land where the sun beat above the jungle canopy, the dead tree gave no shelter from the monsoon, and the cricket no relief from hunger, coming up the Brahmaputra valley to Imphal and its forts by the lake. There was land to be won and lives to be lost. The land where I learnt not to duck a rifle round, as once you heard it, it must have missed. The land where I learnt not to get angry that someone was shooting at me, as it was not personal. The land where I did not hear the hot metal that tore through my flesh and took my heart – not the beating organ but the life I was to have with you. The land where I experienced the chaos of the war, a chaos that created a sense of lack of control that drove some mad and led to many strange superstitions. But for me, the chaos gave me a kind of freedom knowing that my destiny was out of my hands, knowing that there was no point ducking when I heard the crack, finally understanding the universe was indifferent to my fate. There were times when the situation looked desperate, when even the sergeant major looked worried; these moments would sometimes provide a type of euphoria. Moments when you would realise that Death was near, and there was little you could do to influence his decision. Times when trying to deny him his sacrifice would only anger him more and hasten his sword.

One morning, we awoke to find that the enemy had somehow moved during the night, like the tide up a shallow creek, and we were surrounded. We could hear their urgent, whispered conversations metres away, not understanding a single word, but grasping the meaning of every conversation, in the thick, disorientating jungle. They were in between us and the rest of our troops. We all knew without the need for discussion that if we stayed still, we would be discovered and killed – there and then, or more slowly elsewhere. The only thing to do was to move with speed and fight our way back through to our own lines, a course of action that would most likely result in our deaths, but the only course of action that offered the slightest chance of survival. We knew the likely consequences, but knew that was what we would do in unison, as if one mind across the many tired bodies, without a word having to be uttered. In a desperate situation, we accepted what we could not control and took the one course of action that, although likely to be futile, gave us an element of mastery of our destiny. It would at least allow us to own how our story would end. All but one made it back through to our lines that morning. Geordie, who had a fiancée waiting for him in Durham, whose photograph he kept in his left boot, did not make it. I close my eyes and see his lopsided grin and hear his soft accent. I imagine the children he could have had and the grandchildren he would have played with as the old man he never became.

I now realise that the jungle was a nightmare from which I am still trying to wake: a past that is still my present; although I am now many miles away, I never really left. Like so many others who returned, unable to pretend we don't know that death is imminent at any moment, I became frozen in time by guilt and the alienation of this realisation, more than any physical pain I had suffered. Back then, I was a young man with a rank and someone waiting for me: someone who waited for me, but could not be with what returned. The other memories I return to: memories of you. You and the jungle: the times that shaped me the most, are the memories that are clearest. But you never forgot me either. Our eyes met all those years later, you, the poppy girl, outside London Bridge Station. You were still my Irish love, my Isolde. I think you pretended not to see me, but maybe you had seen my face a thousand times before on the shoulders of others, and you were not able to distinguish me from apparitions of me? I looked like an apparition, in amongst the other ghosts in rain jackets, battered dust jackets of books no longer read.

I try and remember why I pushed you away. I told myself at the time it was the physical injuries I returned with, and the consequences of those injuries, what I could no longer do, which I could not ask you to suffer. I supposed the life you would want to lead with the family you were meant to have. Maybe it was not the physical damage, though, not what I was now physically lacking; it was something else. Was I afraid of you? Was I afraid that through your patience and understanding you would come to understand me and at that point I would have seen myself reflected back? Or was it all an excuse, and really what I was afraid of was loving you completely, loving something so much that I knew I would eventually have to lose, having seen so much loss, so much reality? Whatever our life would be, it would end the same. This does not end well. I have seen how it ends. But I couldn't see that you represented life, and I chose death. After seeing what I saw along the mountainous jungle ridges, I couldn't hide from the realisation that I would lose it all, that we all lose it all eventually, so I chose not having anything to lose. I try and remember, but I cannot. It was someone else who made that decision for reasons not clear to the 'me' walking away from the café planning my next operational pause, thinking of something to do that isn't bathing my veins.

As I think back to that foreign land, I think of what I learnt, sheltering under the shadow of that red rock, as hell broke loose. A heap of broken images and confused shouts clutter my mind. 'Stand to! Incoming! Push on!' I think of the nicknames, the laughing, the swearing, the trying not to cry and the surviving. Out of the sun in the shadowed dust, I saw him die. I saw the fear on his face and held his hand. He clung to my hand as if holding on could prevent him slipping into death. A moment seemed to be an eternity, then time stopped completely for him; his hand went limp, he passed on, the fear went and the chaos continued. He would return to the fertile soil on which he lay. Hopefully we would be able to return afterwards to bury him properly and mark the spot. For a moment, I experienced a form of euphoria. I was filled with a mania of both joy and rage. I then dusted myself down and re-joined the battle. In every lull when his face would return, I turned away and thought of you. I clung to your memory like the scent of the sea on the fresh northern wind. In the hot jungle, I remembered the smell of your wet hair the day I bought you flowers, and we got caught in the rain. You cradled the flowers in your delicate arms and rocked them from side to side as we ran through the rising tide. At that moment, I saw the future you wanted that I knew on return I could not give you. Where are you now, my poppy girl? Every November I walk through London Bridge Station hoping to see you there again on the concourse, but each year the bright, blood-red flower offers no promise of resurrection, just eternal sleep: Greek offerings to the dead. But if next year comes again, I will hope to see you, when I see the replica Papaver rhoeas of Flanders field we used to remember. The flower now used as a symbol of peace whilst half a world away, today's soldiers destroy the Papaver somniferum that offers a different, more temporary peace in a new war, in an old place we have been to before.

Lest we forget – that's what we say. But it's not what we do. We forget the lessons we learn in blood and in the aftermath when gifted with hindsight. Those who bear witness are left as an inconvenient reminder to us of our own potential for barbarity, the fragility of our fate and our hubris, so we forget them, too. We bury them deep in our consciousness while they are still alive. We have to forget the witnesses before we can then forget the events they witnessed and the truths they exposed. So, when the guns fall silent, we encourage those who fired those guns to do the same. All those minutes of silence – what do those not there think about during them? We leave it to latter, unaffected generations to honour them, once years of dust have settled, filling the open mouths between tombstone teeth, and scars are healed, with solemn ceremonies. We start to venerate and then celebrate our martyrs who died at the hands of their martyrs. Those who were not there try to remember, while those left who were there are still trying, but failing, to forget. The only ones who seem to forget completely are those who make the decisions to send more to their deaths. They forget the ebb and flow of our follies, one damn thing after another. They allow the flow of blood into fields of future generations, trying to write their names in history by chiselling the names of others onto never-ending walls of remembrance.

My eyes are failing, and I know less now than I did then. My memory is going, but I know the last thing to go will be those images I want to forget first. Stills taken from the film of my life placed on the mantelpiece of memory. Dead eyes staring back at me, devoid of something that had been there just seconds before: memory becoming the corpse of my experience. I thought the grains of sand were units of time, but they might be units of memory. The fear is that my body has more time left than my mind, and the flow of unconscious that defines itself by its memories, as much as its current capabilities, will run dry. My vision retreating, a reaction to what my eyes no longer want to see. At some point, I stopped being who I am and started becoming who I was. I don't want to live in a world where the human body, and by extension the soul, is reduced to nothing more than matter that can be manipulated and mined like the bare earth, even if scientists tell us that dumb matter is all we are at the end of the day; the end of our days. We might not be able to exist in a world like that stripped of our comforting illusions. We put such a premium on 'truth' when there is nothing to say that the 'truth' may not be something we can cope with. Luckily, we can choose not to be what we are – we do so every day when we interact with each other when we see each other as individual people with feelings, imaginations, likes, dislikes, hopes, fears, morals and memories. But I don't interact anymore. But then again, there can be too much communication these days and not enough communion.

I slowly walk to my bus stop; the less time I have left, the slower I am able to move. I wonder how you move now, where you move. Do you still dance like we used to? My eyes make out a garish neon sign. 'Madam Sosostris, clairvoyant, as seen on daytime TV'. The rest of your life mapped out in just ten minutes; maybe I would only need the one minute. We had visited such a woman before we were sent away – voluntarily, as I said. Back then it was in a room above a shabby pub in the East End; a Romani lady using an Egyptian tradition. Devil's picture book spread out in front of us as we tried not to laugh. I asked if she had the gift of augury as she sneezed over the cards before shuffling them, but my question fell on deaf ears. It was Alfie who had convinced us to go in and the first spread was for him. 'The Wheel' and 'The One-eyed Merchant'. 'Here', said she, 'are your cards'. She turned them silently whilst looking me in the eye. 'The Man with Three Staves' is then followed by 'The Beautiful Lady of the Rocks'. The last card was 'The Drowned Phoenician Sailor'. 'Fear death by water', she told me. Look at those pearls he has for his dead eyes. 'The Hanged Man' was in all of our spreads, but went unmentioned by Madam. We thanked her, through smirking mouths and left, stifling schoolboy laughs. If I saw her now, I would not laugh. I would tell her that the last card was not for me. I will not die as a sailor. That was for another one of us. In the inferno, fortunetellers have to walk around backwards, heads twisted around to face the wrong way, preventing them from being able to see what is ahead of them. It is their punishment for their attempts to see the future: a punishment for trying to ape the gods. Some of us have done the same to ourselves, heads turned back focused on a point in the past slowly retreating away from us, but retaining its pull nonetheless.

I continue on to the bus stop, crossing the road as a gang of youths approach, pushing and goading each other, speaking a language as impenetrable to my ears as the English of Athelstan would be but English nonetheless, filling the pavement with puffed out chests and peacock hair. I used to frown at shirts not tucked into trousers, now for this generation trousers hang below underpants. They look angry. They always look angry these days: small lives with big frustrations. Did you have children? If you did, they would likely be older than these youths, by some years now. I wonder: would they have your eyes, your smile, your laugh? Would I recognise them in the street? Today everyone is told they have an equal chance at greatness; there is no glass ceiling now, whoever you are at birth. When the majority don't achieve it, they have no-one to blame except themselves. I think I would have more in common with Raj, my Bengali man, than with these youths. Raj, with his uncommitted head wobble, rather than either a nod or a shake, and his spicy odour and strange lotions. Loyal Raj, who sometimes I thought I had more in common with that not, and then he would do something completely alien to me, which seemed so normal to him. Something rooted in his culture that had never taken hold in mine; not better or worse, just a different equilibrium: an equilibrium that I was threatening. I wonder if he is still alive somewhere, what he makes of the new generation of

Indians and how much of his culture remains. I don't get angry anymore. Anger is for those who refuse their fate, those who have not given up the fight.

I still look for danger up in front as I make my slow bounds, evaluating every bit of cover from view and cover from fire I could take if an enemy appeared after all this time, always knowing whether I would need to move forwards or backwards to make that cover. A half-formed plan I know I would follow without thinking as the first rounds cracked and thumped. One must be so careful these days, just like my days in the east. I do now what I read the poet did after his war: I try to get through things 'somehow, anyhow, in the hope they would mend', but they never do. This city is now unreal to me. The city in which I have lived my whole life is a foreign land to me now. I have The Knowledge; I know its bones but the new flesh is alien to me, and it is adorned in brighter colours and bathed in unusual smells.

Resting against the bus stop, I watch two rock doves perform the same mating dance they have been urged to perform for centuries, and for a moment the man-made sounds of the city are drowned out as they dance their timeless dance. When we danced, the rest of this world did not exist; there were just your eyes looking back at mine, and the music that felt like it was speaking just to us in a language that used no words, but whose meaning was clear. I could be watching them at another time, when the only cliffs they nested in were not artificial ones the city made from the erosion of money and men, but the bare rock precipices of nature hewn by millennia of weather and tectonics. Another time that was before we began to write our history, but after history had started to write itself on each of us. Stripped from the city, their distinct purple and turquoise necks become exotic. I tap my feet to a tune we used to dance to as I watch these birds do their dance, wondering if they hear music like we do. The *Columba Livia* breeds all year round, but now is really their season; they are generally monogamous like us, generally. I have been faithful to you all these years, even though there has been no 'us' to be faithful to. Faithful to our memory – I guess. They, the pigeons, have been observed mourning dead partners and apparently attempting to mate with the dead. I am not sure if this is a confused response to being faced with the mortality of a loved partner or less spiritual and more opportune necrophilia. I hope the former, but maybe the latter is less painful for them, and my hope is a selfish one. They share the incubation of the yet to be born squabs, both parents taking it in turns to sit on the two white eggs that comprise each brood. Both parents then produce milk for them to feed. When I was in India, I used to watch the Sikhs feed the pigeons to honour one of their warriors, and other groups feed them to care for the souls of their departed ancestors. Most dwellers of this city call them 'rats with wings' and wrongly accuse them of spreading disease. We judge so much and know so little.

When I dream in the fits of sleep I get, it is a London of many years ago that I wander through. Back when the fog was brown on a winter's dawn, but it's not winter, it is a summer's dawn I dream of, a dawn as light as midday. The normally busy streets of the city seem deserted and eerily quiet. I am always heading to London Bridge, I move down King William Street, and it is there that I meet a crowd flowing against me, all men, each man with his eyes' fixed on his feet as he shuffles forward. They are all lost souls; they are the dead soldiers from all the wars. I had not thought death had undone so many. This is where death outnumbers life, but no fury smites the air. I never reach my destination as those who I once knew step out of the crowd to fill my pockets with handfuls of dust, until I am weighed down so much I cannot move. I am left lying helplessly on the cold, dry slabs, at the level of the rats. I then always see Stetson, whose hand I had held. I notice the elastic band he always wore around his wrist. With time, I remember more of what he was like when alive, but every memory ends up returning to those dead eyes, those eyes that changed in an instant, and when I call out to him for help, he cannot hear me, and it is those dead eyes that see through me as if I am the ghost.

Soldiers from more recent times are slowly growing out of the cracks between the pavement, pushing past the crisps packets and gossip pages of the free papers, set free from their bindings that flap limply like birds from a child's drawing. The uniforms are different, as they are soldiers from many different nations, friends and foes, but the look on their faces is the same. I have more in common with my enemies than I do some of my countrymen. I want to join them; I want to be back in the jungle, even though I recognise the nightmare that it was. They all have closed fists, thumbs tucked tightly in as they were told to on the parade square, as they begin to march with two-thousand-yard stares; the glorious dead who will never grow old. In those fists are clumps of land from the fields in which they fell; clay, chalk, grit, jungle mulch, grains of dust and desert sand, slowly draining out between their fingers as if in an hourglass. They are all my brothers; they are all the sons I never had.

I wake with no feeling down my left side. Something has changed while I slept. I have no sight in my left eye. The jagged shapes that now dance in front of my unseeing left pupil, in the London morning light, are the same colour of woeful crimson that is left on the earth after men are slain. The shapes break down into red petals that begin to gently fill up my eye from the base, at the speed of blood settling in water. I have a splitting headache, as if a rusty-edged piece of shrapnel is working its way through the soft tissue of my brain, killing those contained only as memories now in the grey matter. I cannot move my left arm or leg. Is this the beginning of the end?

II: A Game of Chess (I)—West London—Summer 2011

I sit here sealed up in this room like the tomb of an ancient mastaba surrounded by all my worldly possessions, as useless to me as if I was a dead Egyptian queen waiting for my heart to be weighed on cosmic scales. Pictures of those I have lost replacing the human sacrifices of that time that used to surround the dead. The chair I sit in, a burnished throne, faces the west and the land of the dead. I sit and remember. I think of my lost loves: the one I had to leave, the other ones who have now left me, gone to the undiscovered country in the west. I think of the man who gave me a child and that child that became a man. I sit quietly. There is no Greek tragedy behind my silence, no barbarous king to be angry at. It is only time I can be angry towards, and time suffers not. My tongue is intact, but there is no-one to hear it wag in this lonely den. But time does not move as it once did, a seabird smothered in spilt crude oil.

Sitting on my chair, I am building a pyre all around me from memories instead of Aeneas' belongings. Who will be sent from heaven to release my spirit and light the fire when it is time for me to fall on my sword? I fear that my body has more time left than my mind, and there will be nothing to release. The flow of unconsciousness that combines my memories and my ability to think in the present that I use to construct what I call my 'self' will run dry, as the memories disappear and my ability to think diminishes. Is anything innate? Does this go as well as all that has been laid upon it over my life? Maybe stripped of all my illusions, the reality that is exposed is too terrifying to contemplate. Or more likely, will I start to struggle to wake fully, never getting past that groggy haze of the first few moments of waking from a deep sleep, remaining in a half world, unable to tell fragments of dreams from real memories, ghosts from people of this world? Unable to shout 'no', as you are unable to move an arm you have slept on, when others stand over me discussing decisions about me, like where I will go to die.

I look around the room at my glittering jewellery, once treasured, now only embraced by the light from the candelabra; withered stumps of time. I smell the slight scent of perfume molecules escaping from the vials of ivory and coloured glass, grains of sand from an egg timer that will never be turned again. The sweet artificial smell mixes with, and then obscures, the natural smell of the room slowly decomposing and the fresh summer air that intermittently pours in through the cracked window pane, which then fails to escape through the coffered ceiling. The breeze ruffles the pages of the piles of newspapers, yellowing from the base upwards as the piles grow like stalagmites towards the ceiling day by day. I am in a broken snow globe that no-one can be bothered to shake anymore. They are all open at the obituaries, the only place I can think of to look for you now. To read in black and white the summary of your life that would omit all the grey of whether you were ever happy, ever fulfilled, ever mended.

There are dolphin cufflinks of dulled brass that were once casually abandoned, but now stand like monuments, possessing a solemn significance given to them by being 'last touched', as if some essence of the person has been left behind on them when all other traces of that person have now gone up in smoke. This significance lacks the adhesiveness of the significance bent into the metal and stone of our permanent, less personal, monuments; the slightest touch could break the spell, like brushing dust from a moth's wing. They would be turned back to everyday objects without meaning; a moth no longer capable of flight that stays clinging to the wall long after it has expired. Oh my beautiful boy – you used to smile when I sang to you. My skin retains no memory of the feel of your skin, my lips no memory of all the kisses I gave you. Is there anything left of you somewhere in this world?

Everything is happening now. All the events of my life as I have experienced them are happening in this present. I am freer in this confusion. There is no nausea-inducing past dragging me backward, filling my head with every selfish thought I have ever had, and, no vertiginous future running away from me, pulling me forward to every end and every future unfulfillable desire. I can remain still, fully present in the now. Maybe my 'self' running dry will be a release: the disintegration of ego into the infinite will be the end of my suffering. I will become all instead of one. I will run empty to become fuller than I have ever felt in life, perfectly connected to all. I will be free from being painfully aware of the passing of time, feeling the blow of every tick and every tock.

But then I remember the aphorism carved into the desk at college in sharp lines shallowed by years of accumulated dirt:

Vita brevis,
Ars longa.

Life is short and art long. The day I read it, life seemed long: a road stretching into the future beyond the horizon and my sight. Looking back now, from the horizon, the road seems short. What have I created that will live on when I am gone? I created a life; I brought a being into the world, an emptiness to be filled. And I watched that life blossom. As I watched, my faith in the world was restored, seeing the childish, pure altruism before the rest of us had our chance to repress, distort and accentuate. But that life has ended now, breaking the natural cycle of life by ending before mine. Grandmother dies, mother dies and then son dies; that is the way things should be. Memory of one is passed to the other, so their stories stay alive. The living can murder the dead a second time, by killing the memory of them, or the living can save them. Who amongst the living will save me? But then what needs saving if there is no 'I' left to save? There is no stage of my life I would wish to return to though, no moment I wish I was back in that could be relived, as it would be someone else reliving it, some younger me that is a stranger to me now and is no more. All of the past happened to someone else, I visit the past as a visitor; I stand as an observer watching the younger me, not within that mind.

It is overcast today and I feel low, the weight of the sodden, unexpected clouds weighing me down. I now fear the stretch I do first thing in the morning that used to be a pleasurable greeting to the day. Sometimes now I lie in bed, just listening to the wind in the leaves and listen to hear the birds as long as possible before my conscious forces itself to try to remember who I am, where I am, what aches and who is no longer with me. I remember the sunset that filled the room last evening, or maybe it was two evenings ago, and how the beauty of it had made me smile. It was not a material thing like the carved lapis lazuli nightingale broach brooding with neglect on the chest of drawers next to the pile of unsent letters, all unsent to the same addressee. I was the only person dead, living or to come who was in this place at that time and was able to witness what I saw. When I go, it is as if that sunset, as I saw it, would have never existed. All those elements came together at that one point in time and space and then came apart again; a breath exhaling, emptying the lungs, allowing you to then breathe again, as the sun will rise again the following morning, as it will the morning after I am no more, also. There is so much beauty in our universe that is not witnessed at all, but the suns, stars, moons and planets keep moving.

I hold my breath until I feel faint and the tingling panic arrives, and then I slowly breathe out, unable to do anything else. As I am low, I start to think in binary again. I think of what I have lost rather than what I had. I sometimes feel, when I cannot help sinking that low, that now there is no-one who knew me as I think of myself, instead of the old lady I am now, left alive; it is like I don't exist already before I have died. Perhaps it is not that binary: existing or not existing. Not all the elements that had to come together for me to be are there now, some have already been exhaled; the rest of me must now go to allow for another sunset. I feel like I will just at most become a minor detail of history – a line in a register, robbed of my personhood, which will disintegrate like a dead dry leaf in the first winter wind. I will just be a name, dates or maybe a flat image staring out of a photograph, waiting in vain for the living to look back. Some photographs will never be looked on again. Of those who will, there will be many where the subject is not known to the viewer, the viewer will look into the eyes of the subject only knowing that no matter how full of life the subject was the moment the photograph froze them in time, they would now be dead. At some point there may be no-one left to look at the unknown dead. All my moments will eventually be lost in time, like my tears in the rain that day you refused to fight for me anymore, but then so will everyone else's. What remains? Even Ozymandias, king of kings, who believed all would despair at his might, only left a lifeless pedestal in the lone and level sands. Nothing beside remained. The sands of time will not need to cover any colossal, and there will be no traveller from an antique land to keep my name alive, even as a precautionary tale.

Then there was my wedding night, a night I did not think of you, more his friends than mine, but I felt like a star, cheeks burning brightly, dress reflecting the lights; sunshine dancing through leaves. There was nervousness and then a small amount of joy. After, there was a honeymoon, so far ago now, tagged on to a business trip to buy cheap wool for his business. The bare, river-scarred and wind-brushed steppes of Patagonia, under skies where the fire-eyed diucon flew. One day when he was meeting local, heavily mustachioed, sweaty businessmen with eyes full of lust at one of the farms, I asked to be taken to see the cave paintings I had heard about sitting at that carved desk, before I had met either of you. The second cave, 'The Cave of Hands', had stencils of human hands in black, white and a red only just distinguished from the red hue of the rock, that were over seven thousand years old. Hands saying, 'I am here'. Almost clambering over each other vainly, trying to get someone's attention, to get someone to acknowledge them, but I could not acknowledge them. One can draw a line around a hand, but not a soul. Where is the substance to trace? I thought I could not know anything about the owners of those hands, other than they once existed. I could not know what any one of them was like, what they believed in, what they loved, what they feared. I thought no-one could now know. They left no words to describe their lives; standing in front of the dry, red rock, their stories seemed to be dead, yet they influence me now sitting here so far away from them in time and distance. I feel them now in the room; their passing allowed all that is here now to come into being, and their presence is still with me. It is not as individuals I feel them, but their collective existence. It is that crooked timber of humanity I feel swaying in the breeze.

A humanity that has emerged through the sum total of people's interactions with each other; a humanity that has emerged as people weave their stories into the frame story, the fiction of the inner stories revealing to us the truth in the outer story. It is a story that has no beginning or end, as long as we are.

I say my name out loud in the quiet room, the sound of my voice increasing the feeling of emptiness, but at the same time giving me strength: I am still here and the strangeness and beauty of that fact pulls me up a little. I am still here. I laugh out loud and the noise of it pleases me. You used to make me laugh before you went away.

I look over past the piles of newspapers to the dust-covered, oak bookcase. Even Shakespeare, whose magic words rest on my shelf, knew the limits of his legacy;

'If thou didst ever hold me in thy heart absent
thee from felicity a while,
And in this harsh world draw thy breath in
pain,
To tell my story'

The great storyteller—a most famous name and stories we know so well—but whom we know so little about. His stories will be remembered as long as there are people to remember, but what will they remember of him? A Polish musician bequeathed his head to the Royal Shakespeare Company to be or not to be used in a production of Hamlet. He has always wanted to play a role and in death asked to play Yorick – maybe in death, I can find the confidence I lacked all those years ago when I was asked to play Mary in the school nativity play and despite my trembling, no words would tumble out. Every night of that run of the play, Hamlet would ask his skull, 'Where be your gibes now?' We know more about that Yorick's skull than Shakespeare the person. His art may have lasted, but it gave him no immortality. When, in his final act, his shipwrecked magician asks on his behalf for a sign from his audience that his work had not been in vain and the art he had created would live on, I believe this was out of a concern for future others, not a belief that it would preserve his current self. His art was for him in his lifetime. Through it, there would have been a joy in its creation, a joy in the interactions with others it created, including the breath of his audience in his sails, and maybe a joy in leaving a gift to others yet to come; he knew his art would give him no pleasure after he was gone.

He knew he was no closer at the end to revealing the answer to our condition. He hoped he had shown us that we all suffer the same from being in this condition and further, that we are all ultimately asking the same questions. In ascetic contemplation of his words and his timeless insights, he has left us a gift that enables us a temporary escape from the striving. I run my pale old hand over the cold, leather bound cover after closing it. Sitting here alone in this room, there is little striving I do these days. When unable to contemplate any more, it is thoughts of you I return to. Your face comes into view, although I have no idea how you would look today if you are still alive. Having your indulgence would set me free; you should have been my audience and I yours.

Even if we knew more details of who was the person capable of such insights, no biography could allow us to really know him across all this time, like the way I came to know you. It could not describe his laugh so that you would recognise it in a crowded room. It could not describe what I saw when I looked into your eyes as we whirled around the dance floor in flat, black words on the flatter white page. We tell his stories, but they are not his now; they are ours, for a time at least, and then later they will become someone else's. They have become stories within our own stories. My story will become someone else's story, too; the self I have created will go, the performances are gone forever and I am already left alone on the stage. But, I told my story like the bard did, and with him but not you, I created another story and saw it through to its end. Now I must leave the stage empty for the next performance.

We need to see an empty stage is not an emptiness of loss, but one of potential, infused with performances past, awaiting the next performance, the contingency of it thrilling and not terrifying. I remember when you were away in the east, a visit to see Mother's friend having her second chance as an actress in the West End, as the blackout restrictions were being lifted. I remember the exotic foreign accents, the cabinet ministers, the spies and the rich, all dining together on meals unaffected by and drinking in the air raid shelter, with lush curtained cubicles with beds, in the pink room of the Savoy, where we stayed that night; but more than anything, I remember the electricity of the empty stage. As Mother and her friend chatted in between the matinee and the evening performance, I walked across the empty space and felt its energy flow through me. I remember that the play was raising money to buy theatrical equipment for soldiers at the front. Money to buy instruments, costumes and props to help soldiers stage their own performances on the fighting fronts and prisoner of war camps across the global theatre of war. I had thought of you watching – you would never have been on stage – some bawdy comedy with men dressed as women that might be interrupted by an enemy barrage and feeling helpless at the absurdness of a world where two people, who just wanted to be together, were forced to be so far away from each other. Back on my empty stage, I listen to myself breathing in and out in the quiet, and my spirits slowly lifting as the darkness falls.

I am not afraid of no longer being here; it is not a long hoped for calm, but it is not now feared. Like Lucretius, I am puzzled how when we are so untroubled about our pre-natal non-existence, we worry so much about our post-mortem non-existence. My non-existence for all the time before I was born does not bother me, so my impending non-existence after my death should not either. I am afraid of how I might die though, what mechanism Atropos, the oldest of the three sisters, will choose for me before she cuts my thread with her 'abhorred shears'. I pray for something quick, ideally something I am not even aware of, but not even the gods can rule over the Fates.

I hear the floorboards of the stairs creak with the memory of footsteps of those departed. My memories are now the flickering shadows on the cave wall, pale imitations of the people and the things that created them. Time suffers not, but my mind does. 'We are dying every day', and as I lose my memories, bits of me really are dying every day. I wish I could light a fire and feel its warmth on my skin, and see you dance in the shadows, and taste the champagne bubbles escape up my nose. We used to dance, the room would spin and my head would, too. I will put on some music and see if it makes the memories clearer, the notes forcing away the fog. I lament their passing, but the pain is mine, not theirs, and like Laelius that should be of comfort.

Time may be running quicker now than before; all of us poor creatures immersed in it are oblivious to this fact, the fact that to some observer outside of time our lives will be over sooner. Perhaps time flows through us rather than we are in its flow. When we are full of life, it can pass slowly through us, but as we become emptier, it starts to move more quickly through us until it flows no more, like the final rushing grains through the timer, without a tick or a tock. I am a time traveller now, but travelling in one direction only, back to when we thought we had all the time in the world, back to a time when we would travel into the future together but just as an observer, always an observer.

My spirits are lifted, but my nerves are bad. Yes, bad. I see you there in the corner of the room through the mist at the edge of my vision. Stay with me. I call out to you, but realise that no-one is there. No-one can hear me. I hear the rustling of blankets in the cot, but I am mistaken. The ghost I see the most is you. I saw your ghost at London Bridge, your apparition, standing, watching me and smiling. I always ask you to speak to me, but you never speak. Why do you never speak? What are you thinking of? I never know, I never knew, what you were thinking. You never wanted to talk about it to me, did you? I would ask you what you were thinking about when you stared out the window, but you always replied the same: 'Nothing'. You murmured in your sleep about the 'rats' alley' where you saw the 'dead men lose their bones'. Maybe they were taken away to the boneyard and piled up like human scrap. I thought then that you did not trust me, but later I realised you just did not know the words. If we cannot find the words, it is hard to share.

'What is that noise?' It is just the wind under the door. 'What is that noise now? What is the wind doing?' It is never more than that. Sometimes I think I hear a baby cry, my baby, but it is nothing, again nothing. The lady comes once a day, but she has to fight her natural recoil that those still so full of life and too busy to contemplate the opposite have for us; those who are near death. It is as if we are somehow contagious rather than just a reminder of the most basic truth; us the old, the ill, the broken. She talks at me, and I try to keep up. I have to keep up. I cannot trust her.

Where are you now? Are you speaking now? Did you ever speak? Not to me, I know that, I think I know that. Do you remember me; do you remember us? Sometimes I think you really did die out there. Something in you definitely died. I would angrily ask you: 'Are you alive, or not? Is there nothing in your head?' I think my little boy needs me, but I am not sure where he is, where he is.

I reach across and put on an old tune; I almost forgot I was going dancing. I always remember the words when the music starts. When I close my eyes, the music makes the memories seem clearer. I see us moving in time with the music and in time with each other. We moved so quickly then. And we smiled. I smile now. I understand the music more now than I ever have; I get lost in it and forget there is a 'me' listening to it. Before, I was too conscious I was listening, thinking 'I am listening to this music', which meant I could not really be listening, letting it enchant me.

Sometimes I feel like what I imagine drowning must feel like. I feel the pressure of the water all over my body, seeping into a sinking ship; I cannot breathe, all sound is distorted and my vision is blurred. Other times, I am just a small pebble dropping into a pond, sinking with minimal resistance, leaving no trace. Occasionally I feel as if I am breaking the surface, like I have tonight, and I can take another breath of air. Suddenly everything becomes clear, before I fall, exhausted, back beneath the murky waters to the world of the drowned sailors with their pearls for eyes, all of us falling slowly towards the locker or the green. I feel myself falling back now. When I wake tomorrow, what will be left? If when consciousness resumes more memories have gone will I still be me and if not, then who?

What shall I do now? What shall I do? I shall rush out as I am, and walk the street with my hair down, and find the nearest dancing hall. I will meet you there, and we will dance till late and our feet ache. What shall we do tomorrow? What shall we ever do? We used to play chess; not you, my husband and I. Quietly moving the pieces with their lidless eyes and limited movements, all except the queen. We were never in love like I was with you. He was a good man, and I miss him too, but I miss the things we did less than things I never got to do with you. I will sing a lullaby that will help him sleep, it always helped him sleep. I wait for a knock upon the door. I cannot just sit here, though I need to be self-sufficient or they will take me away. She will tell them I am a danger to myself. I feel the water closing above my head and feel myself sinking deeper than usual; the pressure increases, my ears begin to hurt. Sounds become more muffled, and it starts to get dark. When she comes tomorrow, I must come up for air. I will try to wake early and look my best. Others may call too, although I don't know who. Hello? Is there anyone there? No, it is just the wind again.

II: A Game of Chess (II)—al-Basrah—Autumn 2005

As the darkness covers the land, we the remaining Ma'dān can
uncover ourselves and speak words we would not dare let the
sunlight hear. We become visible again until daylight makes all
candles superfluous. Our nights are now long. Nights are only short
for those who sleep soundly. But they say it is darkest before the
dawn. I pray to Allah, Glory to Him, the Exalted, there will be a new
dawn soon. I pour myself more tea. I am with child again, Allah be
praised, it will be a son, so I am sitting watching the other girls dance
around the CD player on the weaved-reed mat. Three mosquitoes
mirror their dance around the light. I am with child, and yet Ali is out
running around with the soldiers; soldiers that our Hazab tells us are
now the enemy. The same soldiers, whose inhuman silhouettes move
around in the darkness, and who descend from their monstrous
vehicles and enter uninvited into our homes. The strange monsters
we used to be told about in the marshes that stalked across the

bewitched isle of Hufaidh, whose shores could not be broached without causing madness, come to life wearing uniforms. The same soldiers, who speak in foreign tongues and are now moving towards the village; Nazim has just entered, he must have been up on the roof again, telling us he sees lights heading this way. The Mahadi don't move at night like that in this area, it must be the foreigners blundering their way towards us.

I tell the girls, who are giggling in a collapsed heap after the last song has finished, to turn off the CD player, dim the lights, blow out the candles and hold their flapping tongues still in their heads.

'Ali will be annoyed if we are all here when he gets back'.

'He can be annoyed all he wants. He who wants to his home to be the *mudhif*.

'Ha—what celebrations will he host here, what disputes have been settled?'

'Anyway it is not Ali, it's the British soldiers'.

I turn and look at the picture of him in his *keffiyeh,* standing with his father and uncle in front of the reed wall of the mudhīf. It reminds me that he used to be good looking, with his fine dark moustache, strong hair line and thin figure. I used to say *Ya'aburnee* and kiss that photo, when he was away. 'You bury me', a declaration of my hope that I wished I would die before Ali, so I would not have to live with such loss. But then, as the soldiers invaded our country, I repelled Ali from my heart. It is dangerous to be in love when there is war. I remind myself I am angry at him, and then the thought of how he has lost that figure adds fuel to the fire of that anger.

He who puts his father's customs and feuds ahead of our future. He, who puts his own hate of the dog, who drained our land and scattered our people in all directions as if a skunk had sprayed them, above the future of his own children. Ali talks of how we raised buffalo and cultivated rice, to the rising and setting of Pleiades, and, Sirius which would be reflected in the dark water. He talks of hearing the crying of geese and the croaking of frogs, the sound the canoe made through the water, and the crimson sun setting through the smoke of burning reed beds. He never mentions the bilharzia, the malaria, the droughts and the flooding. I remember more than anything the wind, cold off the water in winter months and spreader of dust in the summer. I remember the sense of being surrounded by water even when it was out of sight, comforting for some, claustrophobic for me. I know now how ungodly we were, but I am sure I sensed this then too. The girls do not know that Ali is working with these soldiers. He may even be approaching with them now. He tells me that these soldiers will help us get our way of life back. He can get them to see our enemies as theirs. He can get them to settle the blood feuds of his father. But, as the daughter, I am the *shaykhah*; unlike me, my father the *sheik* had no sons. I say cast off the anchor of the past, we must look to the future. I pull Nazim close to me, my hands resting on his small but already strong shoulders.

'I don't mind not being able to be out at night now. My father never let me out at night anyway. It is the rubbish that is everywhere that reminds me, even when I don't see the soldiers, that we are living in bad times. I would rather they cleared the streets than gave me a vote I won't be able to exercise freely'.

'It is not being able to get my perfume anymore that bothers me, some days I cannot bear my own smell'.

'Neither can we', which is followed by giggling.

'I miss living under a dictator who hated us; we had so much more freedom then!'

I hush them again. In truth, I do not mind the restrictions, even the veil. It shields me from the lustful gaze of the young men of the marketplace, whose eyes roam the black fabric hoping to find flesh. Beneath the robes I could be a date or a lump of burning coal. I shudder now when I think of the first time I saw the naked flesh of a fisherman standing shamelessly in his boat at midday. A new order will replace the old; the dawn is coming. We can forget the misery from where we have come and move out of these dark times. I will endure more misery in the present if it means my children, some yet to see the light of the day, can live in a better, more secure world, a world I hear described from behind the veil every Friday now we have ended our tradition of praying alone. Our evolution on to the land from the water of the marshes must be complete. We must cut loose the anchor of the past, because it is entirely necessary to reach a better future.

My mother is pleased; she was jealous of my freedom. 'No honourable women would work outside the home', she would scold. Nanna would wink at me from the chair behind her. I was always her *Habibi*. She would talk to me about our language of images and read me poems and stories from the old times, not always Arabic or Persian tales, but tales from all over. For her, though, the images were more real. Her senses blended together so she would taste letters, hear shapes and see numbers as colours. For her, Tuesday was blue and the number five was blood red. It is hereditary. My mother never had it, but Nanna knew early on that it had skipped a generation and I did have it. I don't see colours in words or numbers, but for me sounds sometimes create colours and shapes before my eyes. It is one reason I watch them dance. A dog barking can be blue rapid zig-zags, a ring of the telephone yellow triangles of all sizes rising to the ceiling. My first memory of it comes from when I was seven (green to Nanna). I pricked my thumb and screamed. As I screamed, a rainbow of fireworks shot out from my mouth and bounced off the walls. In the marshes when I used to hear singing drifting across the water in the dark, as I lay on my reed mat, I saw colours drift across the curved roof of our hut following the words. Through me, my children may experience life this way, but I do not wish that this is so. To Nanna it was a gift; to me it is a curse.

'Hurry, cover up, turn off the lights, move the table back onto the mat! Hurry! Stop laughing!'

They do not know that there are weapons are hidden under the dry reed mat that they have been dancing on, and that I used to sleep on many moons ago, taken from my father's hut in the marshes back when the fish swam there. Ali does not know either. I must be strong for my whole family. I must make the right decisions. We do not have the luxury of Ali's ideals; his belief that deference to ghosts of the past will secure our future. The foreigners are not strong enough for this fight, they will talk and then they will leave. Their mothers and their wives will demand they return home. The first voices in the chaos are always the voices of men; it is only when the voices of women are heard that we can find a way out.

The Mahadi sense it is their time now and our neighbours will ensure it is. If we are not strong, the Fedayeen and their al-Qaeda brothers will return after the occupiers flee. This is as clear as honey, yet Ali does not see it. When people see a strong horse and a weak horse, by nature, they will like the strong horse. We will help them end this conflict and then shape the future in peace. What wouldn't a mother do for her children's eternity? Like a doctor in a morgue, we are used to death now. Before we would die by chance; now we live by chance, and I will not be able to watch my children grow up under these conditions; I will die with worry. Like the delicious birds that arrive every winter from the coldest climes, we will hunt them all winter, and those that are left will return home by the spring. Their deaths are justified by what ends we seek, and we have the divine on our side. When the ends are Allah's ends, peace be upon him, all means are surely justified? I can accept their rules and customs if they get us that peace. The more I think this way, the less I see the colours and the shapes. It is only occasionally they come now; when I hear the children sing, I see faint rainbows of teardrops floating past my eyes. Nanna once told me that her mother had a condition which caused her to experience the same sensation that another person feels. If she saw someone touching their cheek, she would feel the same sensation on her own cheek. If she saw someone was in pain, she would feel that same pain. She, too, saw her difference as a blessing. The less I feel apart from our neighbours, the more I feel like I have a purpose. I am sure the full extent of that purpose will soon be apparent. N'shallah.

They are coming here! They are stopping outside, hurry, hurry! Allah, keep misfortune from our house. Keep the infidels, who will struggle to keep their tongues that will be lolling with lust in their open mouths, from breaking down our door and desecrating our home with their dirty boots and their dirtier dogs.

I pull on my veil and detach myself from the world of bodies and colours. I feel safe and ready for battle. Through the veil I see my sisters do the same as one. All veiled, we become one unified force. I am free under this veil; I am not following rules or restrictions as some say. I am following God's will, so I am freer than anyone trapped under the illusion and arrogance of belief that they have the choice how they should live.

That word in our language, the language of our prophet, may Allah honour him and grant him peace. The way I used to feel that way about Ali, but now I would bury him for the sake of our children's future. I would kill him first as well if I had to. Gently and with love, but in these extreme times, I must be prepared to take extreme steps to secure the futures of my children; Allah's children.

'Hurry, hurry!'

There are bangs at our door: a black, gloved fist on the soft metal. With each bang I see an orange dot flash before my eyes, large at first, but quickly contracting to a point. A voice that is not Ali's calls to us through a megaphone in a language I have learnt through pop songs, songs that did not use these harsh words. It is a voice whose tone betrays the nature of its request. A guest should not arrive unannounced at an inconvenient time; there is no requirement to host graciously such a guest. I will not be a gracious host.

'HURRY!'

Allah, may he be glorified and exalted, protect us.

III: The Fire Sermon—Winter—al-Basrah 2005

I can see the river through the tent flap, which is fluttering half-heartedly on the limp breeze we seem to get round about the same time every afternoon at the moment. It is technically not a river but a 'shat', which I am told by Ali means stream. I see the broken hulls, the rust the colour of autumn leaves, whose progress to the bottom of the oil-skinned water probably initially so rapid has now stalled. I am told that this city was broken before this war came, but the evidence of that is now hidden by this new conflict. Detritus of one war covers the detritus of the last, all piled on top of the detritus from the many civilisations that have come and gone in this ancient land. Everyone keeps banging on about how ancient this place is, as if we need to be extra careful when we are smashing the place up with heavy weaponry. Ali, our interpreter, can tell us which war did what damage, but it all looks like one shit heap to me.

The river bears no empty beer bottles, plastic sandwich

wrappers, supermarket trolleys, cigarette butts or other testimony of summer nights, like the canal that the house where I grew up backed on to did. There is no shagging in the bushes of its banks either. There is no shagging here at all. Our rules of engagement speak of protecting life, but for the most part, all we do is take life and have our lives taken, no-one is creating it. A rare, stronger gust of wind makes the tent flap violently, before it moves silently on across the land ignoring all the chaos of men.

I just didn't want to die in the first few weeks. I would have felt that was embarrassing, not that in reality I would have felt anything at all. I am a sergeant now, a man to look up to. I got through those weeks pretending I knew what I was doing, and now I think I do know what I am doing. What I need to do to keep me and the men alive. Anything else is a bonus. Not the sort of bonus those back home are used to getting. They who sit in the city, across the river from where I grew up, taking risks with other people's lives, trying to sound like something they are not by using the language of our profession. Those who grow pampered beards to hide the unisex nature of their roles. The men look up to me as I did to my NCOs when I was as wet behind the ears as they are. That said, some are on their second operational tour already, and they are only just out of their teens. It took me significantly longer to get the experiences some of them have already got. No matter what, I feel I need to pack it away and be strong for the blokes and also the missus back home. I try not to think of her and the kids—it is impossible not to, but I limit it. I email once a day and call every few days when we can, but I don't do video calls like some of the lads do; seeing them is too much of a reminder that life goes on elsewhere when I am stuck here in limbo. I need to stay focused.

The only time I am really scared, not that you would be able to tell, is whenever I get into one of those mobile coffins; the sand-coloured Land Rovers that the corps has decided are suitable as the main mode of troop transport round the area of operations. I fear that moment of heat at my back as an unseen Improvised Explosive Device or 'IED' rips the vehicle and all of us in it apart, exploding the red phosphorus grenades in the pouches of my webbing and removing my flesh from my bones, creating a scene from hell of limbs, hissing red smoke and acrid smells for those in the vehicle behind to deal with. The mortars and rockets fired at our base nightly I fear less, even when the limited ability of the canvas tent roof to protect against a direct hit is considered. 'Big sky, small mortar', my old company sergeant major used to say. It was in the South Atlantic that he experienced his war. He had told me that there, mortars often did not explode on impact in the soft mud – this would whilst not killing anyone, provide what he called a fifty pence/five pence moment, with the two coins representing the two sizes that a particular muscle when contract and expand to in rapid succession on experiencing this near miss. At one time he was all I aspired to be.

A rat creeps softly through the vegetation, dragging its slimy belly on the bank. I lift my rifle and follow it through my sights. It continues on, unaware that I could take its life at any instant, like one of our targets being tracked by an American drone in a cloudless sky.

I scan the horizon through my sights, stopping briefly to look at a couple of birds perched on distant power lines before moving on. Some of the lads have made a rod and have started to fish in the dull canal that breaks from the shat and flows under the wire of the base. Trigger, the youngest recruit in the troop, walked past the tent opening, rod in hand. 'Trigger, you hosepipe, where is your body armour and helmet?' He scuttles back in the direction he came. He is a good lad, but at times I worry that he is depriving a village somewhere of an idiot.

Attacks in the day are rare, and tonight, rain is forecast, which makes an attack unlikely; they don't seem to like going out in the rain. Beyond the city limits is desert. Nothing, except the reason everyone says we are here: the oil fields. I am not really sure what change the season brings here. I know it will get slightly colder, but those working in the shadow of those hellish, fire-breathing wells may not notice that change. From the Merlin helicopter as we were being transported from the airport to our current location, as we crossed the desert floor, lifting over the pylon wires before dropping again to the level judged the safest for helicopters to fly, they looked like oversized guard towers for some place you would be wanted to break out of and not in to.

The boss turned to me and said, in that tone of voice he uses when he is quoting someone that I probably won't have heard of, 'Abandon all hope, ye who enter here'. Moments later, the aircrafts' Defensive Aids System, triggered by one of the multiple sources of heat below, deployed a cloud of small, thin pieces of aluminium chaff and the pyrotechnic flares to the left of the aircraft and the pilot pulled us hard right. Those sitting opposite me, including the company commander, lifted off their seats wide-eyed, the panic in their eyes quickly turning to embarrassment. Defensive Aids Systems had not been covered in the weeklong orientation we had received at the airhead and I wondered what else had not been. When we were landing inside the wire of this base I saw the river, sorry – stream – for the first time, as black as tar. My first thought was of the marines who had died on it further downstream during the tempest of the invasion. I then thought of those veterans we met the Remembrance Sunday before we deployed, who had landed in France all those years ago, who had watched the white bodies pile up on the beaches, not having time to help their mates as they pushed on, still feeling seasick from the journey over to take cover, but then having the rest of their lives to think about what they could have done. Lastly, I thought of the soldiers yet to die on this stretch of water, and whether one of them would be me or one of my blokes.

Behind me, in the direction of the city, the excited sound of horns snaps me into the present. That is our life here: daydreaming of the past, imaging what others are doing in the present that we are not witnessing in other places and fantasising about futures that may never come, before being snapped back into the present in a state of heightened alertness. A false alarm and we slip back to the daydreaming. More rarely, some genuine action and we will be operating at the limits of our focus. It is these few occasions, or even the potential of these, that allows us to justify our disconnection from the everyday of home. We cannot be bothered by the trivial here as we have to deal with life and death, even if so much of what we do here is a different type of trivial.

Sometimes, the daydreaming is a group activity for the lads. When it is, it is usually about sex or who would win in a fight between two unlikely figures – such as Ghandi and Stephen Hawking or figures considered nails such as James Bond and Jason Bourne. When the conversation turns to sex, it is about the brothel in Germany during pre-deployment training, someone's girlfriend or wife they all like, or someone's most embarrassing pull on a run ashore back home. It usually ends with someone calling someone else a 'bell end' and at least two people needing to be wrestled apart by the rest. I used to join in with these conversations, but now I just listen in maintaining a distance. I hear Digger talking about the letters that the boss made us all write to our loved ones that were to only be delivered in the event of our death. He describes how he has written in his letter that he wants his ashes thrown in the face of his wife's new man. I don't laugh out loud, even though I want to.

It is my job to keep them active when we don't have patrol taskings from the company, which we rarely do now. From the early days of training on, it has been drilled into to us that we dominate the ground, and we do this by patrolling. Here, we spend much of our time sitting behind the wire. The reason behind nearly everything we do is self-protection, but we are protecting ourselves from people who are only attacking us because we are still here. We dominate nothing from inside our self-made prisons, while outside the wire, long standing scores are being settled and history is being re-written. Sentry routines and other admin tasks keep us vaguely busy, and we train for a couple of hours most days; physical training, weapons drills, first aid and contact drills mostly. I don't want to beast them for the sake of it; I want to keep them rested, but not bored. The longer we are here without incident, the more comfortable they become. The more times we go out and nothing happens, the more they believe nothing will happen on the next patrol, too. It seems to be a part of human nature that we believe what has happened on a few occasions will be what happens on all similar future occasions. Like the turkey that believes the farmer, who comes out to feed him, will always be friendly right up until the day just before Christmas when instead of food it is a knife he has in his hand. Every patrol we go on where nothing happens makes the lads, who have never been in 'a contact' before, more relaxed. I have to keep them focused and expecting to deal with what they are starting to believe won't now happen. At the same time, I cannot over-exaggerate the risks or that will have the opposite effect to that I am trying to achieve. Tonight, though, we are going out on patrol, despite the weather.

I hear the sound of a sociable lapwing. Yes, we are all bird watchers here. One of the boss's heroes, the war poet Siegfried Sassoon, was a bird watcher, so he has got us all looking for a Basra reed warbler, which is meant to be mega-endangered and only breeds here and over the border in Kuwait. There is a bottle of port for whoever gets first confirmed sighting. Apparently, Iraq is slap bang in the middle of some sort of bird superhighway with hundreds of millions of birds migrating each autumn through to and from their winter quarters in Africa. I said after the boss had briefed the multiple on the identifying characteristics of the warbler – it was one of the best intelligence briefs he has given – that we must be some of the most extreme bird watchers ('twitchers' he calls them/us), but he told us that there is a long tradition of danger in twitching. He told us about a couple of British twitchers in the 1990s who strayed into the path of the Shining Path guerrilla group in Peru and were captured and killed.

The boss told me that we only very recently found out that birds migrate. I think he said it was the early nineteenth century, when a stork turned up in Germany with an African spear through its neck. I thought he was trying to wind me up, but apparently it is true. Cracking effort to soldier on like that with a spear in your Gregory. Not sure many of the lads would crack on with a spear through their neck. Man-gina would claim he would, no doubt. Up to that point, people apparently thought that birds hibernated, lived underwater all winter or there was one theory that they flew to the moon. I am sure there will be some things we think now that will seem nuts to future generations – maybe why we came here to fight this war. Why am I, a working class lad from east London raised on the banks of one great river halfway round the world, in this unreal city with these people who could be from the moon? I suspect in this future, there still will be wars though, unless we are not the creatures we are now and always have been.

I think I can hear the sounds of children laughing on the breeze, but I doubt this can be the case. Ali appears at the entrance to the tent and says, 'knock, knock', which he always finds inexplicably amusing. He is eating raisins from his pocket, shoving them into his grinning, fat face. He is always eating something. I like Ali. His father was a marsh Arab, driven from the marshes by Saddam. His father had met early British explorers and administrators and had told him if the Brits ever returned that he should help them. He saw working with us as a way of honouring his father, or so he tells me on an almost daily basis. People here tell you what you want to hear, but it means nothing. I am not sure he feels that he is honouring his father when he is sitting with the lads watching porn, which he does a lot. He has some odd habits – but I am sure he thinks we have some pretty odd habits, too – he probably thinks all the constant washing we do is strange when minutes later we are sweating and covered with dust again. Before we go out on patrol, he always starts telling us a story, but stops three quarters of the way through and tells us he will finish the story when we are safely back behind the wire. He told me it is so we will look after him and make sure he gets back safely so he can finish the story. The boss finds him more amusing than most. I think some of the lads are not that keen on him; they tell him it is his mates mortaring us when we get incoming in the evenings. It is always said as if it is a joke, but I think both parties know there is more to it – a lack of trust borne out of a lack of understanding, on both sides. The boss has gotten Ali to give us cultural lessons, but it is mostly lost on the lads. In a way, I don't want them to get too close to these people. However, when Ali brought in chicken cooked in a variety of spices and herbs, they were suddenly all over local culture.

I walk with Ali. He has heard we are going out on a patrol, which will involve us moving into an area he knows well. He isn't sure it is a good idea to accompany us. I can hear the calls of prayer starting in the city. It is a haunting noise, but one that I now associate with violence and the fading light; the violet hour. As they all kneel down and face the direction of Mecca, we will sit down facing the direction of the operations room map for the orders group for the patrol this evening. I listen to the clipped voices. They follow a familiar pattern; our own language outsiders would not understand. I take notes that I now don't need as I know the drill and I cannot take out on the ground with me anyway.

Coming out of the O group, our taxis are waiting. Their diesel engines are throbbing under metal forged in Birmingham and running on fuel that comes from the ground here, but cannot be bought at the pumps. I have seen long queues of cars outside petrol stations here while oil seeps out of the ground by the side of the road next to the queue. I back brief the multiple using a map spread across the bonnet and we lock and load. The skylight is fading through purple to black and the clouds that will bring the forecasted rain are slowly rolling in. It has always struck me that what we do has changed so little over the centuries. Warriors from the Greeks through all the ages of the British Empire have sat and heard orders, mounted their horses, size nines or mobile coffins and set out to patrol and fight, using tactics if not equipment each would recognise. At the same time, as we load our weapons and complete radio checks, my wife will be picking the children up outside the school gates. But I push the thought of that from my head and focus on checking my admin and then the blokes. Ali is waiting to hear if I have spoken to the boss about him not coming. I had not, so I went to find him. We were heading to his village to hit a suspected weapons stash. We do so few offensive jobs now, it is only usually when IEDs are involved. We are letting the militias do what they want, outside of blowing us up, and they are still doing that anyway. We no longer dominate the ground in the city, due to lack of patrolling, which I can only guess is a political decision as it is certainly not best practice militarily. I found the boss reading a battered paperback on his deck chair in all his kit ready to go.

'Oh Theseus, dear friend, only the gods can never age, the gods can never die. All else in the world almighty Time obliterates, crushes all to nothing…'

I had heard the name Theseus before, he was the fella who killed the Minotaur, but I was not going to give him the satisfaction. The boss came from a vanishing class of people that believed a point only had real value if it had already been made in some Greek myth.

'I have no idea what you are talking about, boss, and your pocket is undone',

'We good to go?'

'It's Ali's village, so he doesn't want to come'.

'How's your Arabic?'

'Shit',

'Mine too',

'Tell him he can remain in the wagon, and we will put a hessian sack up he can remain behind. Anyone we need to question, we can do it in the wagon'.

We had been talking about the helicopters that ever so occasionally pick us up. Debating how much of the original helicopter remained and how much was now black masking tape. The boss told me it was like Theseus' ship that was preserved as a memorial to his achievements, but over time it rotted away and eventually every plank was replaced, leading to the question, was it really still his ship? I told him it was like the broom a road sweeper had in a sitcom I used to watch; the broom had had 17 new heads and 14 new handles. Apparently over a period of seven years, every cell in the human body is replaced. I have been many different people throughout my life. I had thought about this when I thought about how I would be changed by this tour. I thought about it when some of the blokes spoke about their mates who had lost limbs, and more, on previous tours. Would I still be the same person when I returned?

I visited the military rehabilitation centre at Headley Court before deploying to visit some blokes that I knew from the corps who had been injured on previous tours. They had been some of society's fittest, but were now some of society's most disabled. Some of them had survived injuries that their predecessors in earlier conflicts would not have done — a result of modern medicines' drive to preserve life whatever the quality. I watched them painstakingly re-learn to walk and carry out tasks we take for granted. I stayed over. In the evening, we played Twister with some of the nurses; the game where you have to move parts of your body to different coloured spots on a mat according to the spin of a wheel. It was designed for people who had connected limbs; the injured lads had an advantage, which they made the most of. They removed artificial arms and legs to move them without having to perform the contortions the other players had to do laughing as they did so. When I needed to go for a slash, I asked one of the blokes where the toilet was and he pointed out the toilets there were ironically big enough to run around in.

One of the injured was a young officer called Marcus, who was using the inside of his artificial leg as an ice bucket for his bottle of beer. He chatted to me about how he made it back with all his limbs but a secondary infection meant they had to cut off his left leg in hospital in Birmingham. He told me how arbitrary it seemed where they drew the felt tip pen line across his leg, marking which bit of him he would keep and which bit he would lose. He told me he had three more lines drawn over the following six months as they failed to contain the infection.

'I realised I did not have an emotional attachment to the flesh. I stopped worrying about what I could not control and focussed on what I could—namely how I dealt with it and how I acted', Marcus told me in a slightly slurred voice, talking at me, but probably really talking to himself.

If you reduce it all down to elements and atoms, or whatever they now think are the smallest bits of stuff, how do you draw a line around what needs to be included to make you the same person? You take a map of all the atoms, or whatever unit you like, in the universe at a given point, as we are all apparently made up of the same stuff, and then draw a line and say these however many atoms are you and the rest of the billions are the rest of the universe that is not you. Is it just a group of simple atoms in the brain where the person is? How do they create what is thinking about that memory now as I walk across the yellow sand? I turned round the corner of the line of tents, and I found Ali holding court telling a story to the rest of my multiple.

'This tale is about a Persian king and his new bride. The king discovers that first his brother's wife has been unfaithful when he was away on tour and then that his own wife has also been unfaithful. What is you say Man-gina: 'snakes with tits' I think? Anyway, he executes his wife and decides that all women are the same and none of them can be trusted. No longer having any faith in women, he begins to marry a succession of virgins, only to execute each one the next morning, before she has a chance to dishonour him. Eventually the vizier, whose duty it is to provide new wives, cannot find any more. Scheherazade, the vizier's daughter, trying to help her father offers herself as the next bride and her father eventually agrees. On the night of their marriage, Scheherazade, who was well fit by the way, begins to tell the king a tale. So she began, "A fisherman discovers a heavy locked chest along the River Tigris–"

'Not too far from where we are now', Ali interrupted himself to say.

'And he sells it to the Caliph, Harun, who has the chest broken open, only to find inside it the dead body of a young woman, cut into pieces. Harun orders his vizier, Ja'far, to find the murderer within three days or else Harun will have him executed. Ja'far fails to find the culprit before the three days are up. Just when Harun is about to have Ja'far executed for his failure, two men appear, one a good looking young man and the other an old man, both claim that they are the murderer. Both men argue and call the other a liar, as each attempts to claim responsibility for the murder and then cutting the woman up into pieces. This continues until the young man proves that he is the murderer by accurately describing the chest in which the cut up woman was found. The young man reveals that he was her husband and the old man her father, who was attempting to save his son-in-law by taking the blame. Harun then demands to know the young man's motives for murdering his wife. The young man then begins his story.

'He eulogizes her as a faultless wife and mother of his three beloved children, and describes how she one day requested a rare apple when she was feeling unwell. He undertook a two-week long trip to Basra, where he found three such apples in the Caliph's orchard. On his return north to Baghdad, she tells him that she could no longer eat the apples because she was feeling too ill. So he returned to work at his shop, annoyed at his wasted efforts. Then he notices a slave passing by tossing one of the rare apples from hand to hand. Asking where he got the apple, the slave tells him that he received it from his girlfriend, who had three such apples that her husband had given her. The young man is now understandably convinced that his wife is being unfaithful. He rushes home, and demands to know from her how many apples she still has. He discovers that she only has two so proceeds to murder her. He then describes how he attempted to get rid of the evidence by cutting her body to pieces, wrapping it in layers of shawls and carpets, hiding her body in a locked chest. He then abandons the chest in the River Tigris. After he returns home, his son confesses to him that he had actually stolen one of the apples and that a slave had taken it off him and then he had run away with it. The boy also confessed that he told the slave about his father's quest to Basra for the apples, before he stole it. Out of guilt, the young man requests Harun to execute him for his unjust murder. Harun, however, refuses to punish the young man out of sympathy and instead sets poor Ja'far a new assignment: to find the slave who caused the tragedy again within three days, or be executed—again. Ja'far fails for a second time to find the culprit before the new deadline. On the day deadline expires, he is summoned to be executed. As he bids an emotional farewell to all his family members, he hugs his beloved youngest daughter last, who is sobbing uncontrollably. It is then, by complete accident that he discovers…

'But then she stops. She tells the king that she will continue the story the following evening. So when he awakes the next morning and his executioner arrives to conduct his usual duty, the king…

'And I will tell you the rest when we get back in, boys. Off we go now!'

As Ali stops, the guys groan and then all mount up. I tell Ali that he is coming out on the ground with us, which I assume he knew already due to his storytelling, but that he can remain in the wagon behind a hessian sack with his balaclava on. He shrugs and makes his shambling way over to the boss's Land Rover. We all mount up, complete final radio checks and push off – me in the passenger seat of the last vehicle map out on my lap and the boss in the passenger seat of the first vehicle. My driver is Man-gina, the oldest in the multiple to still be a marine, so named for his party trick of concealing his cock between his legs when drunk. His extra experience gave him a good sixth sense for trouble, which is why I had him as my driver. As the wife probably pulls in on to our gravel drive at home, our wagons roll out through the chicane of oversized sand bags, past the Challenger II main battle tank, out in to Basra, into the red zone, past the wire that separates them from us, into the brave new world we have created for them.

The job was a dry hole. Of the few jobs we do, most of them are. There was no-one there to take off target in blacked out goggles and plasti-cuffs and process at the detention centre. Someone we could pluck out of their world in the middle of the night and hold in limbo, where there is literally no time, no watches on the guards, no clocks on the walls and constant artificial daylight. I tell the blokes that even a tiger fails in eighty percent of its ambushes, but it does little for the low morale, which is growing day by day as the reason for us being here becomes less and less clear. I tell myself that we do this to keep my girls safe on the other side of the world. The house tonight was full of women and kids. They looked at us like we were rapists. One of the women spat at the boss and seemed to wave the sight of him from her eyes as he tried to speak to her. We represent things to them that we would be horrified to be accused of as individuals. It is an odd feeling to be hated by strangers who do not know you. A few weeks back, we were tasked with providing a cordon for a groundbreaking ceremony; we were going to be sitting ducks. I suggested to the boss that we inform the ops room that someone approached us when out on patrol and warned us that the cordon to the ceremony was going to be targeted by a sniper. I thought this would pull the plug on it and therefore avoid putting the blokes at risk for the sake of trying to prove to the world that things were getting better here and it had all been worth it. He did not hesitate in his response. He told me that we could not put ourselves above the mission. In the end, it was cancelled anyway, as various local VIPs could not agree on who would do what and stand where.

In the rain on the way back from the dry hole, our vehicles got stuck in the mud. The lads got soaked piss wet through lying prone around the stranded vehicles while we waited in the dark for the QRF to arrive. This was the main route into Basra from the east, yet no-one else passed us for the hour we were there waiting. In the past, there would probably have been fishermen heading to work on the oily shat around about this time, heading past us deeper into the heart of the darkness, but not now in these uncertain times. Those that can, leave when war comes; those that cannot look with envy up at the sky, to the birds that move on whenever the environment is no longer favourable and the weather turns.

I jump into the back of the boss's wagon to find him sitting there chatting with Ali, waiting on an update over the radio of the ETA of the QRF, who has still not shown up. I know it is not good drills to be sitting in the same wagon as the boss like this out on the ground, but the rain, the dark and lack of any sign of life give me the confidence that a brief catch up will do no harm. Ali is telling the boss about the early gods of this god forsaken place. I enter to hear Ali telling the boss: 'Enki stands at the empty riverbeds and fills them with his "water", as he is known as the lord of the waters and lord of semen'. We might as well be wanking in an empty river bed all the good we are doing here.

'My wife calls me an infidel when I talk of the older gods rather than her newer god'. Ali went on, 'He also told man about the impending flood from the gods, telling one bloke to build a boat to survive it'.

The boss seemed to find that amusing. I have spent most of my military career hearing people steal each other's stories, so was less amused; stories get recycled, each teller spinning his own take on the original so much so that no-one eventually really knows where most of them come from and whose they really are – like the boat or the broom.

As dawn approaches, I can hear the wail of the mosque begin, which is sparking a second chorus of dogs barking. What was dust earlier that evening was now a muddy paste that was caked over everything. We are finally moving again after the QRF arrives and eventually pull us out before managing to get stuck themselves, leading to us then having to pull them out. The blokes in the back of the wagon have dismounted and are walking in front of the vehicle as we cross the bridge over the shat that will take us back into the city. I remember noticing the cracked nail on Man-gina's dirty sausage finger as he pushed and pulled at the stiff steering wheel, which in turn eased the wheels of the wagon into line with the rickety wooden bridge across the Shat al-Arab. The small details you remember after the event. Then there was jarring violence and bright light, followed by the gentle sound of thousands upon thousands of water droplets returning to back to the shat, from where they had come from only fractions of seconds before – or did I imagine that as my ears must have been ringing at that point? I think of seeing fireworks at night over a distant harbour, then nothing; complete silence.

Oil on the surface is burning. The ear is burning, sounds are burning… the nose is burning, odours are burning… the tongue is burning, flavours are burning… the body is burning, tangibles are burning… the mind is burning, ideas are burning, consciousness is burning… nothing will be the same again… nothing.

IV: Death by Water—al-Basrah—Spring 2006

In terms of ways of dying, I would have taken an Improvised Explosive Device any day of the week. It would be over quickly, I probably would not even know about it and it would be unlikely that any tactical error was to be blamed; you can do everything right in terms of tactics and drills and just be in the wrong place at the wrong time. I knew it was low risk down here in Basra compared to Baghdad, but I feared death by the blade of the terrorist knife – all filmed and broadcast so everyone who ever knew me could watch my brutal end. It was not a fear of knowing my death was coming, but rather that everyone else would somehow look on my life as defined by how I died, the whole of my life being seen as tragic due to the last few moments of it. I have heard some say you should not judge a life until it is at its end; some that you should not judge a life until after it has ended. I am not sure about this, but what I am sure of is that the method of your death and the last few moments of your life should not define how people view your whole life, even though this seems to be what happens time and again. The military has always instilled in me that you should be judged on what you do rather than what happens to you. Others cannot take a good life away from you. I still would not want those I care about to see me die. I would want them to know what happened to me, but seeing it happen would be too much. With a bomb, I would not care that my body was ripped to pieces, no-one back home would see the details and I would most likely feel nothing.

At least I had confidence that my family would know what had happened to me, not a given for soldiers in the past. From what I have read, heard and experienced to an extent, there is a powerful fear that soldiers from all ages have had of leaving this world with no markers, with none of their loved ones knowing what happened to them. My old sergeant major told me of the Argentine prisoners he dealt with in the Falklands, some of whom had letters home stuffed deep inside their pockets; others who had their next of kin details or home addresses written on their arms in marker pen, or had made makeshift dog tags out of card. I have read that in the American Civil War soldiers would write their details on small pieces of paper that they pinned to the inside of the back of their overcoats, which would often be washed away by any rain. The end is important to us, even though I say it's not. What are they all afraid of? All these soldiers seem more afraid of what might happen after their death rather than death itself. Afraid that no-one would know their fate. Afraid that their loved ones would not know and would be left wondering what happened to them. The people who make others disappear, do it not just to avoid the unwanted attention a dead body generates from authorities, but because they understand the pain and fear it creates. The 'Disappeared' become symbolic to every conflict, their fate worse than those of whose tortures we know. People whose stories are never known to those that care about them, making them stripped of their personhood.

Even those who don't believe that the body is needed again in some sort of afterlife and know that the person who used to be that body is gone find it hard to not care what happens to the flesh left behind. We were shocked when we saw the bodies of American contractors carried through the streets in this conflict; shocked and then angry. I see it all the time in the lads – even us soldiers who are meant to be calculated, disciplined, rational agents– knowing something to be the case does not necessarily change the way we emotionally think about it, in fact it rarely does. Knowing that prepping your kit in a certain way won't affect the chances of surviving a patrol, nor will the order in which you neck your breakfast. We all know we will risk life to get a fallen comrade back even if they are already dead. It makes no sense, but none of us will question it.

Whatever, I never thought my death would come in the water. Nothing flashed before my eyes; there was no trip down memory lane of all the stages of my life. For me, there was no memory download, no desperate attempt to find something useful to help. The only cliché was time did slow; every second seemed like a minute, each minute an hour. I remember feeling a sharp pain above my right eye, seeing bubbles of air leave my mouth and slowly rise through the blood and the water to the surface and then a brown hand pushes through, grab hold of my webbing and pull me free from the water. I later find out it was Ali's hand. I burst the surface as I hear the cries and distant sirens. My ears are full of noises; my right eye is filling with blood. I hear the boss's frantic voice on the radio; I realise that I have never heard him shout before and I hear sirens in the distance that will be turned back when they understand who has been hit. I don't hear Man-gina's voice at all. I somehow know he is dead. Seconds ago, he was alive, and now he is dead. He was a good soldier, a real fighter, but he has, as we all will in the end, now lost his fight. All of us officers, NCOs, marines and soldiers die; there is no rank in death. Even generals die – they just get to do it when they are fat, old and probably rich. All the things he worries about don't matter now; they have melted into the air as has the flesh that will have been stripped from his bones. All the memories he held within his head are gone. How many others who were being kept alive in his head perished at that second, how many events and interactions were now as if they never happened?

I feel the jab of the morphine pen in my thigh and feel my veins fill with the poppy tears. I feel like I am drowning again, but above water this time. I am able to hear the cries and see my injuries by the erratically roaming torch that briefly gives the impression I am in a sticky floored nightclub, knocked over by a drunken punch rather than the explosive punch of an Improvised Explosive Device. I no longer care about either the cries or the injuries. I know I will live, and I feel no pain. Those here now will remember those that died here and us the injured. Those in the rest of the battle group will turn away from our memory as they do not need to see what could be their fate at least till the end of the tour. Our bed spaces will be cleared quickly, boxed up and sent home with what is left of us. They will all move on for now; they have to, what else can they do? They cannot stop and reflect that the messes we have become were once fit soldiers like them. I drift in and out and out again of consciousness. There is a figure over me in silhouette – everyone looks the same in silhouette in all the kit we wear. I think it is Dinger, the team medic. I tell them to move on to the others, but I am ignored. I know they must be dead if he stays with me.

I remember the noise of the helicopter and being hit by the dust and God knows what else which was being blown around before entering the vortex of hot air caused by the whirling blades. There was frantic activity next to me; people were working quickly, shouting to each other, urgently trying to be heard over the noise of the rotors. I think I remember seeing a pair of eyes rolled back in a head, completely white, like a pair of pearls. It is difficult to distinguish between what I remember and what people told me happened afterwards. I felt a lifting and then we were moving forward at speed, and I still did not care what was happening. There were lights and more noises and then darkness as I sank full fathom five into something that did not feel like sleep or any other state I had ever been in before.

V. What the Thunder Said—London—Summer 2011

After the torchlight on red, sweaty faces, the shouting, the crying and the cold silence of the icy opiate in my veins, there was the long agony. And then there was being stuck in a prison which was meant to be a place of rehabilitation, but in reality it was a place where I succumbed to the soldier's disease: morphine addiction. I lost two years of my life drifting in and out of an opiate haze as they have tried to deal with my injuries, which at first had seemed so superficial. I watched up close the medical professionals pushing the injured out of the valley of the death, those that would have in previous conflicts died on the battlefield, to the top of the hill and physical survival. I was never sure whether they honestly thought that they were really fixing these soldiers or whether they knew all the time that, disease or maybe even the unseen mental scars would drag them back down to the valley floor at some point, despite everything that they had done.

Eventually, I went back to Headley Court, the mansion,

hydrotherapy pools, gymnasiums and workshops for prosthetics in the high woods. This time, though, I went back as a patient rather than a visitor. Everyone is home now from the desert; the last boots have lifted off the sand; the sweat has dried; the thirsts that were built up in the dry lands have now been quenched. Everyone has had time to stop and think. The conflict in Iraq, for the British military anyway, has ended. For the people of Iraq, it still rages, mountains of bodies are still piling up and the thunder of bombs break the temporary silences of city market places and villages of mud-cracked houses. For those of us injured, there are still battles to be fought. The rest of the brigade came home, and then have now deployed again to what we see as a new war and the locals see as round three. A war that is still raging after a spring offensive, over distant mountains, providing a new influx of patients. I am no longer with them, my beloved corps, although some old friends have found their way here in recent weeks. My war is already beginning to be forgotten. Man-gina is still dead and he is being slowly wiped from the memory of many who knew him. I battle to stop my memories of him fading. He was once like me, and I will one day be what he is now.

In the early days of the uber-excessive drinking – I am down to just excessive now – I would get filled with rage. I wanted to avenge those responsible for killing Man-gina. I wanted to hurt them and let them know why they were being hurt. I wanted to attack all those who supported his killers and attack anyone who did not understand the sacrifice he had made for them. I shouted at office workers in pubs who were going on with their lives as if he hadn't given his life for them. I swung wildly at students I overheard sanctimoniously judging from the safety of a chain bar happy hour. I stared aggressively at anyone who looked remotely Arabic. The rage slowly turned inwards and mutated into a self-hatred of the pathetic creature I had become. I became a pathetic creature that did not deserve the love of my wife and girls. I have somehow pushed them away, though I am not sure how. I had thought many times about what physical losses I could cope with, what I would prefer to lose and what I would keep; lose a foot, keep a hand, but I never thought about what this would be like. I never thought I would be crippled by these unseen injuries that don't show up on any MRI scan.

The boss visited me early on. He looked like shit. When I told him this, he shrugged rather than give me any sort of comeback that I would have expected. The rest of the tour and then the first days of his post-operational tour leave had left its mark. I tried to crack a few funnies about the state I was in (worse than after a night out in Newcastle etc.) and he tried to smile, but he looked like he was finding it hard work. He told me about his visits to the families of those that had not made it. 'All those broken lives and for what? What were we trying to do; what were we thinking, interfering in all these people's actual lives for the sake of finding out others' poorly conceived plans were not based in reality? I thought we were doing some good. It seems so obvious in hindsight to all; we shouldn't interfere; we should stand back and let others kill each other. It is not our problem'. He told me that Ali had been killed too, which I had not heard. He had ended up hanging from a tree after being accused of being a collaborator. He had apparently been tortured before he died. He was left hanging with his eyes and tongue cut out, sign round his neck, for a whole day before the police eventually cut him down. His body was never claimed by his family. The boss told me he thought it might have been as a result of the night we took him to his village. I told him it was unlikely, more to make him feel better. I wondered what story Ali had left untold at the end, and I thought of his family that I had never met.

-|-

'He had to go, his life for the lives of my children and their children to come. As a father, he should have been prepared to lay down his life for his children; he should not have needed me to do it. He should not have forced me to do it. The society we will build here will require more to give their lives, but they will be rewarded in paradise; we will be rewarded and re-united. The Prophet, Peace be Upon Him, showed us that to achieve great things blood must be spilt. He picked up a sword and we must too. You cannot stand by and hope that the world will just work itself out. If you stand by and do nothing, then evil will triumph. I know it was the right thing to do, though I do have moments of weakness when I hope he did not know at the end it was me who told them what he had been doing. I hope the children will forgive me one day. During these weak moments, I worry that the future will provide no more security to my children than the present chaos does. I question how I can really protect them from the flux of life? To hold your breath is to lose your breath. A society based on the quest for security is nothing but a breath-retention contest in which everyone is as taut as a drum and as purple as a beet. I try to silence my head and its weak thoughts with what my heart knows. When I have these thoughts, I see orange and crimson flames dance before my eyes and my skin begins to itch. The flames still dance when I close my eyes'.

-|-

Before the boss left, he told me about a wildlife documentary he had watched the night before when staying at his parents' house—he had split up with his missus since returning so was staying with them while on leave rather than in the empty mess. It had been about some species of geese. He told me that they build their nests high on mountain cliffs, away from predators, but this was a double edged sword as it was also away from any food. Then, instead of bringing food to the newly hatched geese, the new geese chicks have to get to the ground. Unable to fly, at three days old, they have to pin their ears back and bin themselves off the cliff; their tiny size, feathery down feathers and light weight helps them to semi glide down, limiting the impact slightly when they hit the rocks below, but many still get smashed to pieces and die from the impact. He told me how he had watched gosling after gosling bin themselves off and smash into the rock cliffs below. One would hit the bottom and die, then the next one would jump. That was not even the end of it though, arctic foxes are then attracted by the noise made by the watching parent geese and pitch up to capture some of the dead or injured. I knew he was telling me this for a reason, but I was not sure what the reason was, and was not sure he knew.

Since I came off the morphine, I have self-medicated with alcohol, and I have lost more of my life to a fog. I have been wandering round, drowning in the desert, despite having come home. I always went at drinking like I went at being a soldier. It is hard to be at the extreme in one part of your life and for that not to push you to the extreme in everything you do. Previously being a soldier kept it in check, as I wanted to be fitter, better drilled and promoted quicker than any of my peers. There were never any half measures. I wanted to be the best. With soldiering gone there was nothing to act as a counterbalance. I became the best at drinking.

I cannot admit I have an issue, as if I do, then no-one will ever see me the same again. Everyone sees me differently because of where I have been without even knowing what happened to me. They hear where I have been, and then they see my injuries, and they think they know it all. They know it all, except that question they feel they need to ask, that question we all dread: 'have you ever killed anyone?' They don't realise it's not that we have experienced something different over there, that we get exposed to something alien to their lives, it is that being over there showed us the chaos that exists everywhere when the happy illusions of our society are stripped away. We have just visited a place where the surface layer has been eroded and the bedrock that is beneath us all is exposed. Once we have seen this, we cannot again accept the illusion no matter how drunk we get. I am like the turkey that survived Christmas; despite surviving, all I can see now is the farmer's knife.

But if I said out loud how I feel, what I see when my mind drifts, what I see when I dream at night, what I hear when a door slams, I would then have nothing left. The illusion of my mental strength is all I have left of the man I used to be. Much of my adult life, my physical presence has defined me. For the rest of my life, it will more about what I cannot do rather than what I can do. I am a bark with no dog. I do not even have the rank slides any more after my medical discharge. I have a crossed a line from serving to non-serving, I am separated now from those still serving, but I am not a civie either; I am now in a state of limbo, a veteran. If I admit I am weak, I would cross another line. I would become one of the blokes who could not handle it. I am not one of them.

-|-

This is no place to be sick. You need to be strong to survive here. You need to be strong enough to deal with the superbugs, the lack of sleep in the noisy ward, the constant prodding and poking and the unhealthy food. I am still here though, my old bones, still surviving despite it all. Despite the fact I have had a stroke. I overhear the nurses talking about their weekends. They live in a different world to the one I live in. Some of their admissions shocked me slightly. Dr Mitra, who has the same non-committal head wobble Raj had, caught me with a disapproving look on my face the other morning when I was eavesdropping. I am less invisible here than I usually am and I keep forgetting that. But they are kind to me. The more I listen to them, the more I recognise them. Then, one morning, as the first sunlight of the day bursts into the ward, I see one of the youngest nurses combing her hair after her night shift, and for a moment, it is you I see and not her. For days, I cannot get the image out of my head of you combing your hair in the sunlight, despite not knowing if this is an image I have ever really seen. I cannot stop thinking about you. As I feel the ground rush up towards me, as the fall that has been my life reaches what must be the final stages of its descent, it is your memory that looms the largest and begins to fill my field of vision. It is not the fall that kills you, it's the landing.

Dr Mitra is kind, too. He saw that I was uncomfortable when trying to ask him where he was from, despite being certain that his strong accent meant he had grown up elsewhere. When you have grown up all your life in a place, it must quite alienating to be regularly asked where you are from, implying you cannot really properly be from here. I blurted out that I used to know someone from Bengal when he told me he was from Kolkata, as if that would mean we had some sort of special bond. I have not told him where I fought; I don't know how he will react. I don't know how I would react saying things out loud after all these years. Was it really me who went there and did that?

-|-

There is an old boy, Arthur, who has joined our physio group, he too is a veteran. He is an in-patient, whilst I am only an out-patient these days. He is learning to walk again after a stroke; learning with little patience, but good progress. When I first spoke to him, I thought he was either deaf or a bit simple, but I then realised he was just not used to conversation, outside of the transactional. It was hard work at first, but I managed to coax a few replies out of him, and after a while, he would even initiate a conversation. He knew I was ex-military, and the way he asked the few questions he asked as our paths crossed made it obvious he had served, too. When I first asked him directly, he was dismissive of his war, in his rasping, dry-grass voice through stiff lips, waving away the question. He is from the generation where the values and standards I have been brought up on were so much more common: a generation that still wears a suit when they no longer have to work. One day after working together during the physiotherapy session for the first time, he invited me to join him for a smoke outside. He led me through a fire exit, next to a cash point, to a small memorial garden where he made his way over to a dark wooden bench and slowly sat himself down. In front of the bench was a small fountain that had been reduced to a drip by years of dirt clogging its arteries. It became a tradition. We would retreat to our bench and sit in front of the grime-filled fountain that even the birds now turned their beaks up at, seeking less gipping fonts to bathe in. We would take it in turns to buy the tobacco and each roll our own cigarette from it, as we had both done before with other friends in different parts of the world we had been sent to. We would not say much, but felt comfortable with the silences, listening to the drip, drip of the dirty fountain.

One day I told him about my tour, about the explosion, about Man-gina, about the boss and his visit to me, when he looked like shit, and about what he had told me about Ali. Arthur suggested I should go look the boss up. I had assumed he would be okay, but Arthur was right; I should drop him a line and take him out for a wet. I remembered thinking one day, as he was giving orders in front of the multiple, that he is closer in age to my daughters than to me – although I wouldn't want him anywhere near my daughters. After the facts, I told Arthur about how we thought we were in Iraq to make the lives of the people there better, but all we did was cause carnage. I told Arthur about some of the lads who visited me in hospital who had told me similar things about Afghanistan. This was always after they had told me with excitement about the number of contacts they had had and what ordnance they had managed to get down the two-way range. I told him I thought that people need to belong to a specific culture and need to be ruled by people who belong to that same culture. We tried to make them like us, but they are different. The challenge is not to make us all the same, but to learn to live with our differences. He slowly but purposefully nodded. I was brought up by my mother to believe that violence was a result of error or ignorance, and if we educate ourselves, we become less predisposed to be violent (you can imagine how pleased she was when I signed up after I had managed to get into grammar school), but so much of the violence I have witnessed has been the result of people thinking they are doing good with a different kind of ignorance to that my mother was referring to. At the end of our chat, Arthur told me, somewhat out of the blue, that he enjoyed our conversations.

Arthur eventually told me, a few days later, where his war had been fought. I asked if he had ever been back to India. He said he hadn't, as he got too emotional on aeroplanes. 'Besides', he said, 'the ones we were fighting are now in charge. Or they were at least. I don't keep up with that sort of thing anymore'. He said they had killed many of them at Imphal, Indians fighting as the Indian National Army alongside the Japanese. He told me that they had pursued the INA to Rangoon, hunting them as they tried to sow discontent in our own Indian soldiers, like his batman Raj. He told me about the officers they caught that were tried for treason after the war, which achieved the discontent they had been rousing for all along. He told me of the mutinies and the marches which hastened the end of the Raj. He told me about sitting in the back of the divisional operations room and watching as the burly Colonel Slim, with wartime rank of Lieutenant General, would process updates, evaluate consequences and issue orders, all grounded in a reality he himself would witness and influenced by the love he had for his men. But even though his stories were full of the details you could only know if you were there, it was as if he was telling me about an episode of history that happened to someone else.

Arthur did not mention any family to me, although he paused

when I asked him if he ever married. He asked me in return if I had a family, and I said we were separated. He asked me why in a moment that seemed out of character for him, and I told him it was complicated, even though it probably isn't. He looked like he wanted to push me on it, but caught himself, and made an apologetic gesture before relighting his cigarette that had gone out with an old, dented, sliver Zippo lighter that had an inscription on the lid made undecipherable by time.

It was only on about the seventh or eighth time we sat on the bench I properly noticed the plaque. I had seen it the first time Arthur had led me out to the garden, but I had never bothered to read it. I used my thumb to wipe away the thin layer of green lichen, with Arthur watching me.

'Bench sponsored by the staff of King's College Hospital. To the memory and honour of the veterans of yesterday, today and tomorrow'.

The veterans of tomorrow; we will remember, we will honour, yet we know that won't stop there being more. All those generations fighting so the next won't have to, yet they do over and over again. We both stared at it for a silent minute before limping back to the next session. I started to visit Arthur some evenings on days when we didn't have physio together. I liked his unobtrusive company; he reminded me of what I once wanted to be: the stoic warrior.

Then I got to see another Arthur. It had been three nights after riots had broken out in north London after a young black guy had been shot by the police. There were claims he was unarmed when he was shot. Some were claiming a weapon had been planted on him. The local community saw it as further evidence of police brutality and their status as second class citizens in their own city. Two nights previously the, rioting had spread to several other London boroughs. The night before, the rioting had spread to outside London to other cities. As we sat on the bench, Arthur told me the old boy next to him in the ward, with a pencil-thin, white moustache and an equally thin mind, had called them 'new barbarians' and spoke about the 'swarming hordes of hoodies stumbling out of an endless parade of sports gear shops and electronic goods stores'. As they watched the twenty-four-hour news on the muted TV in the ward, with the alarmist ticker tape headlines, he told him that you could tell a lot about these people by the shops they looted. 'There were no bookshops looted', he would announce triumphantly as if this proved his point undisputedly.

- | -

'When I looked at the images on the news from my bed, even though there were many in the news blaming everything from the lack of male role models, aggressive policing, welfare dependence, to claiming the rioters were just doing it for fun, I first thought that it was not the fault of those on the streets, but of the previous generations. Some look at the comforts and leisure time that these kids have now and think them lucky, but the fact that they do not have to struggle to survive in the same way as our ancestors, far and relatively near, is also a problem for them. In its place, what do they have to give their lives purpose? We have not provided hopes and jobs for these young people, we don't offer them the same educational or employment opportunities, we have not instilled in them values and we have passed down no cultural heritage. We have taken from them all that we held sacred, interactions that soothed the soul, and given them nothing to replace it other than the means to provide instant gratification and the restless idea of progress. Everything but the surface of life has been denied to them. We have bequeathed them merely a receipt for deceit.

'We have not given them an identity, and we have not given them a sense of purpose, which can combine to give their lives meaning. At the same time, we tell them that they are living at the end of history, in the final evolution of society, where everyone should be happy and anyone can be whatever they want. Indeed, we believe in this utopian myth so completely, we have spilt blood trying to force it on others. It is a noble goal to be satisfied with mere existence, just being part of this universe, but for many of us I feel an untenable one. They have had a bad deal from us and no-one is listening to them. Like those across the Arab world; they have had enough of their corrupt leaders, who do not represent them. From MPs' expenses scandal, to bankers' bonuses for bankrupting the rest of us, to journalists hacking the phones of murdered school girls; they see those above them helping themselves and flaunting the law. They see this caste of people disappearing over the horizon, so they take for themselves from what is left. The politicians speak of a 'broken society' as if they are not responsible for breaking it. Since the towers fell, we have lost our way. While some have tied themselves in guilty knots excusing the inexcusable, confused about what values need to be fought for, others have continued to fall into a well of hubris, using fear to pull us down with them, trying to convince us that the reflection on the murky water at the bottom of the well we were heading for was daylight. In fortune telling, did you know the Tower card symbolises a catastrophic destruction of a way of life. The memorial they built to commemorate the twin towers was a pair of pits in the ground, pits where we can bury our confidence in the future. For some time, I have lamented on what is lost or we are in the process of losing.

'But when I moaned to Doctor Mitra about this, he looked at me with confusion and told me: "but that is how it must be. The next generation will always reject the current generation as they rejected the generation before them. Towers will always fall and new ones will be built again, and they too will fall sometime". He would then get me to breath in, breath out, breath in, breath out. "See Arthur", he would say as he took my pulse and listened to my breathing, "You need to breathe in to get the air you need to survive, but the moment you breathe in, holding your breath becomes the very thing that will kill you and you must breathe out again to survive. You are always alive and dead, we are always both and never either". He would chuckle to himself and tell me to swallow'.

-|-

I had never heard him speak so much, and he was now in full flow, speaking as if he could not stop himself even if he wanted to. It was like a dam was breaking, water that began to flow in a trickle was now gushing uncontrollably. He kept going as I worried about him running out of breath or having another stroke. The more he spoke, the less frequently he turned his head towards me. The more he got into it, the more it seemed like he was no longer talking to me, but someone else who was not physically present.

-|-

'And Dr Mitra was right. Towers have been built and fallen since Babel. My uncle told me during his war he was posted around the village of Albert at the Somme. His name was Albert too, so he felt like it had special significance to him (we were all 'A's in my family). There was a statue dubbed the Golden Virgin on top of a basilica, which was hit by a shell in 1915 and slumped to a near-horizontal position afterwards. The British troops said that whoever made the statue fall would lose the war, whilst the Germans soldiers thought whoever knocked down the tower would win the war. The British finally destroyed it in 1918, to prevent the Germans from using the church tower as a machine gun post and proved the Germans right, although in this instance, I imagine the Germans would have preferred to have been wrong. There were days on the Somme when Albert said he felt he was witnessing the end of civilisation. He did not speak to me of any of the details, I doubt he spoke to anyone about what he saw, other than admitting his fear that what he was seeing was going to be the end of days. He died a young man of leukaemia, that he believed was caused by the gas, but this was never acknowledged officially. My aunt always said that it was what the war did to his heart, rather than the leukaemia, that killed him. We will now never know. Generations before have thought they were witnessing the end of time.

'I saw the end of arguably the greatest empire the world had seen from a corner of it that people don't now remember. Generation after generation have felt they were on the brink of utopia, at the end of history, only to fall back; the sacrifices they made exposed as the horrific waste they were with hindsight. My generation thought they were fighting so future generations would not have to, yet your generation is still fighting, even in some of the same places. People think I was fighting a great evil, but I was fighting against those who are now heroes in their own land, and the empire who I was fighting for is gone. Your generation has suffered a form of delusion, sacrificing the present for some vague and unpredictable future in a land that has nothing to do with you. Meanwhile, others are yet again fixed on the notion that some splendid future is in store for humanity, guaranteed by history or the encrypted words of sacred texts, which justifies appalling cruelties in the present. All those generations trying to find meaning in the killing: fearing a loss of meaning more than a loss of life. Each generation believing they are making a new world when the sun seems to be forever rising and going down on the same world. Each generation is an end in itself; each life is an end in itself.

'I lost my sense of context. I saw the riots on the streets as the end of all days. London Bridge is not falling down. It is just the end of my days. I wanted to feel like my life was happening at a key moment in history, as if that would give it more meaning. You are the first person I have really talked to for a very long time. The conversations I have had with you these last weeks and the conversations with Dr Mitra have woken me from a slumber. As I have started to gain perspective, I have realised that I had become stuck in the recent past, reflecting on what happened all that time ago, reflecting on what I could have done differently, convinced I was defined by the events that occurred in the blink of the cosmic eye. I realise now that I had become obsessed with preserving something that no longer existed, but at the same time would exist again and again. All the things I could have been I did not become. I stopped living in the now; I stopped my story evolving. As much as I was carrying the memories of all those others, trying to preserve something I could no more preserve than the flesh and bones of the departed, I was also carrying the memory of the man I used to be. I was trying to hold on to that as much as the others. I know now, though that man was dead too. We are not as unified as we think. I now realise that multiple versions of the 'me' have existed, producing a sense of what I think is 'me'. It is sometimes a precarious confederation of 'selves', and there is an ever present danger of disintegration. Our conversations have halted that slow disintegration for me.

'I remember the big counter offensive after the monsoon had broken. We slowly moved through the assembly area to the forming up point, following the coloured lamps that designated the formally bland logistics that led towards the chaos of a dawn attack. We were to attack uphill towards the Japanese defensive positions, at the end of their stretched lines of communication, where the enemy was waiting, starving and as exhausted as we were. As we all, quite willingly, moved towards extreme danger, I noticed that my body started to act independently. As I tried to roll a cigarette, I noticed my hand shaking, yet I thought that I did not feel nervous. I felt the stinging of the salty sweat dripping into my eyes, yet I thought I was not particularly hot, in the relative coolness of the jungle before first light. Others could no longer speak; others soiled themselves. It was mind not having control over body, but it was not just a link being broken by the stress, it was more than that, there was almost a rejection of one by the other. It was as if their bodies no longer trusted the consciousness it had created, and started acting independently of it. It recognised that the mind was not serving its best interests and was placing the body in grave danger.

'Later, during the fighting, I saw in the faces of some of those in my platoon, a fading away of what made them recognisable to me. Left behind was a more basic animal, capable of maiming and killing to survive. Maybe this is why we struggle to talk about some of our experiences as 'we' are not really present during these moments, our bodies having rejected us, taking back over the reins to deal with the danger. What thinks about these things is not the same thing that did these things. This animal sees people as threats, not as people; it has no problem inflicting violence we would abhor. Our culture can do the same. When under threat, it as a whole retreats into a black and white world, where a person or a people become a threat to be dealt with, rather than individuals to be treated as such. Our metaphysical instincts rarely survive the empirical. But we cannot absolve ourselves of blame so easily. What was there then is part of us now. We underestimate the influence and the control that that basic animal has on us. We accept the illusion of our unity and the dominance of our conscious mind, but the animal is always there, in us and the society we build, ready to take back the reins, urging us on, while we come up with post hoc reasons to explain to ourselves why. This creature may be the real us: the only thing that is really consistent about us. It may be the reason for our existence. Our conscious life may be no more than a happy by-product, an evolutionary mutation that may, at some point, hinder rather than help our survival. But that by-product exists and creates all that I think is worth fighting for in this world—it creates people capable of the most complex emotional interactions and expressions. 'We' are not an illusion in terms of existence. Nothing can convince me, that when I looked into her eyes, that there was nothing there but matter; there was a person there looking back and seeing me as a person too, making me a person by that acknowledgment.

'And that's where we must start from: acceptance that we exist as people, not just animals, but not necessarily for any predestined purpose. We must then try and make the best of it, creating our own meaning, and we can do that through the interactions we have with others, who also exist, and we recognise not as just the material creatures we might be, but creatures that have also developed this amazing, unexplained and ever shifting by-product.

'I am not the same person that I was when I looked at her then, but everything I am is built on the shoulders of that man. All these years of living in isolation have made me realise, on my own, there is no way I can say for sure what I am today is who I was yesterday. I owe my existence to him, and I must pay my debts to him and collect on his. Many have speculated whether there is something that unifies all these different selves over time. Whether there is something that makes us the same person, in spite of the fact that so much of what we have done, we don't remember, and so much of what we do seems like it happened to someone else. For those that accept there is, there is much speculation as to what it is that fills the space in-between, what is the unaccounted for dark matter of the soul. There are theories of emergence, of materialism or hardware and software, but for me, they all look in the wrong place. For me, I see that the dark matter of consciousness is not within, but in the space between me and you, the vacant interstellar spaces. What holds us together as people are our interactions with those who know us and love us. We create each other through two-way mirrors. We are all characters in each other's stories. Without you all these years, in my isolation, I have stopped being a person and have become just a passive reservoir of sensations and memories.

'This is why those who lose their loved ones feel the loss as if part of them has died. Why when separated from everyone you love, your mind starts to unravel. This is why solitary confinement works. I think many who face the terror of annihilation, and the prospect of eternity without others, can find that this precarious confederation starts to unravel. When we take action to keep it together, we often have the reverse effect. We shut down, batten down the hatches, shut our mouths to stop the meltdown, to stop the leaking away of the dark matter imperceptible to the human eye, believing it is all inside us, but it's not. We withdraw from others and die some more; we stop rejuvenating, stop allowing new 'selves', which need to fill new moments of the present. Each new self needs to come into being, like each child needs to become an adult. I stopped myself moving on and becoming all the other men I could have been in a lifetime, stopped creating new memories, shared memories with others, who I loved and could have loved me. Memories built on what defined me as me and that would be part of each new me the years would bring: rejuvenating myself out of the soil of experience, new growth from the old roots. Each new me being enriched by the interactions with others, each new me being a part of others too, binding myself to this world and an infinite future presents, becoming more than the flesh and dry old bones, becoming more than just combinations of matter locked in a war of all against all. For each individual self that I am, there is only the present, and I have not been living in it for too many years. So much of our folly is from the quest to keep alive what must die. There is no Holy Grail'.

-|-

This is not how I expect Arthur to talk; it makes me feel uncomfortable. I have not had anyone ever talk like this before to me, even the boss who liked the odd big word and bit of ancient history, but he does not seem embarrassed by my silence. I try to look on him kindly, but to me it all sounds too foreign, too out there to mean anything real or have any practical use. It is detached from how we live our lives. I want to dismiss it and suggest to Arthur that I believe a good drink would be enough to deal with his current philosophical confusion. When sometimes the boss would stray into this territory, I would often feel that it was just a convenient thing to say, as if he did not really believe it down in his gut to be true. It was rather just another story that could be weaved somehow to make sense enough to comfort, but not really be bought in to. However, the boss never spoke with the conviction Arthur is now speaking with. I sit in silence, not saying anything for what seems like ages, but in reality, it is only probably a couple of minutes.

I think of the orange-clad monks I had seen over the course of the last few weeks in the main entrance hall to the hospital. These monks, in orange robes, had been making this picture out of coloured sand by filing down pieces of coloured chalk, letting the dust run down a metal cylinder onto the picture. According to the sign next to them that announced it was part of a cultural exchange programme organised by the local council, the picture was apparently meant to represent the universe and everything in it. I stood watching them one evening after visiting Arthur, for want of anything better to do other than head to a bar. They worked in silence, totally focused on the task, somehow creating this symmetrical picture, which looked like something a computer programmer might produce, seemingly without communicating with each other.

A few evenings after watching them, I walked through the main entrance hall again to find it had gone. I walked over to reception and asked what happened to it. After weeks of creating this colourful, intricate pattern of sand, they had apparently held a ceremony over the finished picture and then brushed all the sand together. They then took it outside to the water feature out of the front of the main entrance and tipped it into the running water in the centre of the feature. All those weeks of intense concentration were undone in a few seconds. The beautiful picture destroyed and just a pile of multi-coloured dust left behind floating on the surface of the water.

-|-

I see the confusion and embarrassment in his eyes, but I don't care. I suspect he wants to tell me to grow a pair, as he does not know of my injuries that mean I do quite literally need to grow a pair, but this is not possible. I am mostly talking to myself, saying out loud things I have been thinking in the quiet of all these years. I will continue, and when I am done, the only thing I need to have convinced him of is that he needs to talk. And I need him to deliver the letters. The letters must get there. I must not forget the letters. It will be my chance to be re-united with my Cordelia. She must know that I still care and not a single moment has gone by over the years that she has been out of my thoughts. She will know that through those letters I managed to retain some of my self.

-|-

There is then thunder, and it starts to rain. The dripping of the fountain becomes more urgent. We move across the courtyard and into the deserted chapel to take cover. I grab his arm as he slips on the wet slabs and nearly fall myself. We support each other, and dry bones push the heavy green door and limp into the accumulated quiet of the chapel, sitting down in a space empty of people, but full of stored hopes for improbable recoveries, pleas for less pain and lamentations for what is lost.

We are silent as the wailing of an ambulance siren draws closer, flashes of blue light dance on the ceiling and through the stained glass behind the alter. He fiddles with the elastic band he wears around his left wrist. When he has caught his breath, the conversation moves on, as a damp gust of wind smashes the increasingly heavy rain against the chapel windows. Now, though it flows less urgently, it is more measured, as if this is now for my benefit, whereas before Arthur had little care whether I was following him or not.

- | -

'Dr Mitra has been telling me about Post Traumatic Stress Disorder; he wants me to talk to someone about what happened to me during the war. He says it is never too late and there is nothing to be embarrassed about. He says there is evidence of Post Traumatic Stress Disorder that can be traced back to 1300BC; accounts of soldiers being visited by 'ghosts they faced in battle' that fit with a modern diagnosis of it. He says that the condition is likely to be as old as human civilisation. Apparently, it is in Herodotus, who referred to a warrior during the battle of Marathon suffering from it. He told me that more veterans of the Falkland's Conflict committed suicide than died fighting at the time. He believes that if some of those who died had had someone to talk to and felt that they could talk, they might still be alive today.

'When Dr Mitra told me of Herodotus, it made me think of the battered copy of the Odyssey I started to read as we set sail from Portsmouth on my way to war. It had been forced on me before as a schoolboy, but this time I read it for pleasure. As I sat on the back of the troop transporter, the wake of my ship became the 'gleaming wake' of Odysseus' black ship. Voices from across the centuries whispered to me from the frothy tops of waves that ploughed the unharvestable, cruel sea in a way they had never done before. I can now see Odysseus' journey after the Trojan Wars as one grand metaphor. As he desperately tried to get himself home to his family, the storms, shipwrecks, vengeful gods, enchantresses, monsters and cannibals represented the pull of the past, and, the consequences of the violence he had witnessed and inflicted. When Odysseus exposed himself to the sirens, strapped to his mast by his crew, the songs they sang were of his own heroic past. They were songs of his adventures in Troy. They wanted to lure him to the rocks with stories of what he once was, they tempted him with a return to the simpler time of war and the company of soldiers he had lost. Odysseus' crew, who had beeswax in their ears so they could not hear the sirens' songs, or his pleas to be released, left him fastened in place, saving him from ruin on the perilous rocks. Odysseus survived his years of wandering by often playing different roles and creating fictions, and, by hiding his scars and his true identity, but it is only after he has been to the halls of hell and back, when he tells his story, and then soon after reveals himself to his son and then his wife, that he can finally overcome the final barriers to his homecoming and be at peace.

'I have been wandering like Odysseus, even though my boat home docked many years ago. My journey is now longer in years than his epic, if not in nautical miles; yet I am still to fully return home. I still long for the black and white of the jungle slopes and cling to the memories of those lost in the sea of that great conflict. Maybe Madam Sosostris was right; lured by the sirens' songs, I will eventually drown in this sea of memories. If I am to survive, I need to stay tied to the present, but I have long been slipping my bindings. Like Odysseus, I need the help of others to fasten me to the mast; I need to stop pretending to be someone else and face forward again'.

-|-

I thought of my old sergeant major, the man I once wanted to be, and the alcoholic he became. He drank himself to death in his early fifties, and I never really spent too much time thinking why. In the same way, I always look closely at any homeless person I see on the streets of London, as I am convinced one day I will see someone I know, but I never really question why I am so certain of this and whether there is anything I can do about it. My old sergeant major was dismissed as not being able to handle his grog; a weakness was implied. To us, normal is coping no matter what and not asking for help. Maybe he used all his energy trying for so long to give the impression he had his shit together that he eventually ran out of energy to function at all. Maybe asking for help is the bravest thing we can do. We all need shipmates who will lash us to the mast when we need them to.

-|-

'I think he is right, and I want to talk to you as I think you need to talk too. I want to tell you that at first I felt guilty about surviving, as well as filled with rage at those who killed my friends. Now it is about not doing anything with the time I felt guilty about having. I want to tell you that when I dream, I still see the faces of those I knew who died and still sometimes wake up and want to cry. I want to tell you that sometimes I am glad it was not me, that it was the others, and that sometimes I fear I am going to hell because I have killed. And I want to tell you that often I want to go back there, to the jungle, despite all this. I also want to say that I will wager any amount you care that I am not alone in feeling these things, in my generation or in yours.

'I have been numb to all that I have experienced for too long. I have had death walking by my side all these years. The Old Testament says each soldier who goes to war must pay a half-shekel to God for ransom on his soul, and each warrior who returns must ask for expiation. My expiation has never been granted. I suppose I never asked. I am asking now. Don't be like me. My generation is held on a pedestal we don't deserve; as if that will make up for the way we were treated back when we needed understanding. People admire us standing stoically, medals on chest, seemingly unaware we are being used as stooges for today's politicians to add legitimacy to their actions. I was not a brave man. Many of my generation were and had to be, otherwise great evil would have prevailed. They stopped evil prevailing, but they did not change the world. We should be wary of marching others off to fight, filling them with hollow ideals, more to do with politics of expediency and dreams that will never come to pass, when they could instead be allowed to live their lives. They instead could be allowed to be all they could be, and help others do the same. They will still, over time, find meaning and undertake actions based on what they hope will survive beyond their deaths, the sons and daughters, legacies of labour and art, but it will not be at the cost of not living their lives.

'Focus on now; start moving forward. That is not to say forget the past; you cannot even if you wanted to, but understand its drag. Tell your family, tell them you are talking to someone and ready to move forward again, if you cannot share with them everything. We are all too wrapped up in our own pain and posterity, but we create ourselves through what we do and our interactions. It is no good scrabbling around in the dark of a prison cell looking for the key; the keys are not kept in the cells they lock. The key will be out there somewhere. When we do nothing and do not interact, we cannot become what we can. We emerge from process and interaction, not a substance. We are a shape the wind makes in the leaves as it passes through'.

-|-

I think back to the rehabilitation centre at Headley Court and those lads who suffered from what is known as something called 'phantom limbs'. For most of them, it was an intense itch in whichever limb they had lost, but for some, it was chronic pain in the limb that was not there anymore. Maybe this is what more of us are suffering from without realising – phantom pains. Pain in a part of us that is not there anymore. As Arthur would say, 'in versions of us that are not there anymore'. At Headley Court when the pain killers don't work, they try mirror therapy. They hold up a mirror in a way that, when you scratch your limb that is still there, it looks like you are scratching the phantom limb. You trick your brain into thinking the itch is dealt with and then the pain goes. It is a simple idea, but the best ones usually are, and it seems to work. Maybe those of us with unseen injuries also need to work out how to scratch the itch and allow ourselves to move on. I have been self-medicating, trying to numb myself with the drink, but like some of those at Headley Court, the drugs are not working for me. I need to try something else. Maybe I need to get someone to hold a mirror up to me, rather than holding up the bottom of an empty glass. I don't get the majority of what Arthur is banging on about, but I think he is right on one thing. I should summon up the courage to talk. I have never had the range of emotions some expect me to have, but I owe it to others to try and do this at least. It is a simple idea, but…

Arthur continues, but all I can think of now is Cathy and the girls, my beautiful girls, and why I have not done what I need to do. I need to talk to them; I need to be with them. I think of all the things I wrote in the letter the boss made us write that they would have received if I had not survived. Because I did survive, they were never told those things; the letter remained unsent. I don't know about some of things Arthur is saying, but why would I now not tell them all those little things that mean so much? I need to give them a chance at understanding, and I need to give myself a chance of living again. I owe it to those to make the best of the time I have left and not give up on the world. What is the alternative? Drink harder and longer? Keep sinking to the bottom, as if I had never been pulled out of the shat? Sinking until I reach a watery grave surrounded by no-one; maybe only found much later in some squalid bed sit, because the landlord of my local pub raises the alarm after not seeing me destroying myself in the corner of his bar for a few days? There would be no flag-draped coffin, newspaper tribute, mention in Parliament, packed graveside or weeping wife and grieving daughters. I will try to use those late night, whisky-soaked words I don't usually use in the sober daylight hours and be better than the man I once hoped to be.

-|-

'We won't live on forever. When our physical bodies end, our capability for creating new selves ends. Slowly, the memories of all of our selves will die out as those who know us pass on too. Life has to end. The fact that it does gives it value. There is only the present, but we need the past and the future to make it all it can be. It is not as cumulative as we think though. From self to self, something is always lost. Over time, we don't become the sum of all we are: one self passes on the story of all those who have come before to the next, and over time, this story suffers the fate of all stories passed on across time and tellers. One day, there will be a version of me that will die, and I hope he does not go through too much pain but dies well. For the rest of us, our job is not to sit back and wait for his coming, but to fulfil each of our potentials as best we can, in the place and the time we live, and to keep rejuvenating. We are creatures that live through stories, but I have become a minor character in my own story; it is time I started being the author and narrator again.

Storytelling is how we process our experiences. We cannot resist their arc, all the big stories we tell ourselves involve the idea of progression; they have journeys where the hero ends up reaching a goal or all of us reaching a promised land. We cannot help feeling like our individual lives should be like that too, and we want to get to the end where something is achieved or reached, all the loose ends are tied up, justice is done and love finds a way. As with many things, even when we know at our core, this is unlikely to be the case; this we cannot help but believe it anyway'.

-|-

He placed the lighter he had been gripping throughout back in his jacket, brushed the imaginary creases or non-existent crumbs from his immaculate trousers and then his sleeves and announced abruptly in a different voice, a voice I recognised from the parade square, a controlled voice that precedes action—

-|-

'I have some letters that I should have sent a long time ago that need to be delivered to a person, who I need you to help me find. I know now why I wrote them, and I know now that they should not remain unsent. I have an address, but she may not still be there, you might know how to find out? I don't honestly know if she is still alive, I may be too late. It is very important to me'.

-|-

The gap between the clap and thunder widens as the storm moves on, having left its rain all over the land, which remains open and moist, sucking up every last drop after a long dry summer. The water seeps into the empty spaces, what is not used will flow eventually to the sea and will be taken up again in the cycle that has been in motion since before we started our crawl out of the oceans. There will be life and there will be growth again.

The next morning, groups of volunteers across the city band together, with brooms, dustbin bags, enthusiasm and the sense of belonging to a community in a place, to sweep up after the riots. Elsewhere, the police make arrests, telecommunications companies shut down media and life carries on for all but a small number, who lives ended over the few days of chaos in this great city on an ancient river. A city that has seen many better days and some worse, a city that once ruled the world, a city that has seen births and deaths of those who have hailed from every corner of the world it once ruled. A city that has celebrated the end of wars and endured the attempts of some to start new ones. A city, whose fabric is scarred with those memories, scars that her inhabitants walk past every day, often without noticing.

VI: After the Rains Have Come—London—The Present

He found her for me, my Isolde. He said it was easy. She was still there in the house she had made her home, although now she was there alone, her family had gone. All this time that has passed made me assume she was so far away that she would have been unreachable, but all that time she was only minutes away. This disorientates me. His wife, Cathy, has taken her the letters I never sent. He thought it would be less intimidating if she took them round. Cathy was eager to help. She now knows I never forgot her, even if she never opens a single letter. She has told Cathy that she remembers me, too. Cathy said she seems confused though; her memory is going. She had to knock several times before she heard a voice call out, and then wait a little longer for her to reach the door. She took Cathy back into her sitting room, where amongst piles of newspapers, she repeated my name out loud several times when Cathy explained why she had come round. She is still there, but it sounds like she has started to leave. She says she remembers me; she said she would want to see me, but what does she remember and who does she want to see – the young man in love with her, the tired broken soldier, this sad old limping man that has succeeded those others?

It is an uphill struggle, but I am getting stronger every day. She cannot leave the house now; she is too weak. The next journey she makes outside her house may be her last. The front door is the furthest she can make on her own, so I have to get to her. We won't get to dance again, but maybe we can still hear those old tunes together once more. I just want to look her in the eyes. Dr Mitra tells me I am pushing myself too hard and I must take it easy and slow down, but I will not. There is now, after all this time, a sense of urgency. I remember the doctors who cared for my sister as she reached the end, who spoke of preserving dignity in death. They mainly meant balancing pain with prolonging life. This resulted in my sister dying addled by drugs and physically incapacitated by the plastic tubes snaking all over her body. There is nothing you can do to give that moment of physical passing dignity. I think of Geordie and Stetson; they died in combat, a death held up as an honourable way to die for generations. What I saw had no honour or dignity – it was just violence, pain and disintegration. I tried to give them dignity through carrying their memory, but I fear I failed them in my impossible task. I know now that the greatest dignity to be found in death is the dignity of the life that preceded it, not in the way you go or how you are remembered afterwards. I think Dr Mitra understands this, and so despite his protests, he encourages my progress. He knows that I won't go gently into the good night. I was a soldier once, and I will fight again to the end.

My anger is back and with it, my desire to fight. I am angry at the time I have lost, the slumber I have been in and the absurdity of it all. In recent weeks, I have also felt a euphoria I felt back in the jungle all those years ago. I have always known that life was fragile and that one day I will die, but I have, despite my experiences, never really accepted it. The fact that this body and all it contains will soon be dead is beyond my control. The stroke has reminded me of that fact. I must let go of any thoughts that exhaust my mind by trying to convince me otherwise. What I can control is where I direct the remaining energy. I can focus on the joy of acceptance, of letting go of all I cannot control and grasping what is left that I can. The joy in realising that, despite it all, I can choose to write the end of my own story, no matter how desperate, in fact because of how desperate it is. Despite it all I have the power to be defiant until the end. This is what causes that euphoria: the mix of joy and rage.

I now understand how my poor sister felt when she found out she only had weeks left to live due to the cancer that was causing cells in numerous parts of her body to grow and reproduce uncontrollably, attacking everything in their path. At the time, I did not understand why she almost seemed relieved. She was angry at the disease aggressively destroying her, but she was mostly calm. A peace came over her as she accepted finally that she really was going to die, like that of a spouse finally caught having an affair, the relief of not having to live a lie anymore bringing a greater peace than the pain of discovery. It seems to also bring a desire to laugh. She was at her funniest in those final days, laughing all the time and making others laugh too. It was the same sense of humour that I had missed since being demobbed. Back in the jungle, we laughed the same way and as often. I remember having to suppress laughter as we rushed through the enemy back to our own lines. It is the acceptance of our fate and the acceptance of who we really are that brings us this peace. She knew there would be no more rejuvenation for her, she could just concentrate on the present and focus on living her final days as she wanted to live. Euphoria is from the Greek meaning the 'power of enduring'. Maybe originally, it was trying to describe the feeling you get when you, for a moment, really understand what it is to be alive at that point in time and realise that this enduring will not last forever. 'The search for origins ends in fragments'.

I will fight until I am finally unable to fight anymore and do it with a smile on my face. I am not sure if old men ought to be explorers, but this old man will be a fighter. This is how I will spend my final days. This fight will be an activity that defines me, like pushing the boulder defines Sisyphus, ancient Sisyphus; the man who defied the gods. He stole their secrets and put Death in chains, so that no-one needed to die. Except you cannot stop Death doing what Death does. The god of war freed Death from his chains, and he carries on with work still today and one day I will be part of his body of work. As Death does what he does, we have to do what we do. As Sisyphus goes about his endless task, we are encouraged to think about Sisyphus's thoughts when he is marching down the mountain, to start up it again. We are told this is the tragic moment; the moment when he becomes conscious of his desperate situation in the brief respite in his toils. When Sisyphus acknowledges the futility of his punishment and the certainty of his fate, he is freed to realize the absurdity of the situation and to reach a state of contented acceptance. He then bends his back once more and continues his toils. We are meant to imagine that Sisyphus finds happiness. I imagine his happiness to be a euphoric one.

It is time now to bend my back once more. I must tell my story and encourage others to tell their stories, freeing them from their anchors of the past or false idols of the future, as I have now cast aside my own. It is how I want you to see me and through you how I want to see myself. The goal of life is life itself. The purpose of the singer is the song, the writer the novel.

I am back in the present, yet I feel like I did when I was back in the jungle listening in the night; I feel free again. I have squandered my most precious possession – time on this earth. I should have shared it with those I loved the most, giving them the greatest gift I can give them, the only thing that really is finite. It's strange that words are so inadequate. 'Yet, like the asthmatic struggling for breath, so the lover must struggle for words'. I will lift my head and look in to your kind Irish eyes one last time and hold your hand at the end, so you know it is me and I have really come back. I will hear you laugh and let you make me laugh. This is what I will do; it will complete our story and determine what I am, and it will allow me to become a full person again before the end. Part of what I am has always been owned by you; I create myself through you. We need to write the final chapter of our story together, it does not matter to me if no-one else ever hears this story as long as we know how it ends. The future will be what it will be; its events are already in time's womb, so I best get cracking: my sun will set with you.

-|-

I am lost in the music. I am not really listening though, and I am just letting it be my guide, taking me from memory to memory, repairing broken links. I want to go to a church before I go and hear a choir sing. I wonder what memories that would stir: the scent of the candles, the still air and the empty echoes. Then the music fades away, and there is a rhythmic knock at my door. A rhythm that I recognise from long ago, but it is weaker now. Maybe it was in my mind. But no, I hear it again stronger than before; there is someone there at the door. And then I hear the wind mimicking your voice, mimicking how your voice might sound all these years later as if it was playing dry reeds with its gusts. The impression is close enough for me to know it is meant to be you. But, it is you. It is not the wind on the reeds. I am scared this is not real, but then I remember that kind lady who came round with those letters, which lie all around me. It is you and it is real; I am sure of it now. In a moment, after all this time, I will see you again.

'Are you there?' Your voice asks again.

- | -

I feel like a star-crossed teenager again. I am the young man whirling you round the dance floor, bathing in the music, everything a blur accept your beautiful eyes staring back at me, reflecting me back, telling me that I really do exist. You are the music while the music lasts. My hands are shaking at the anticipation of your touch, and I have a stupid grin breaking across my wrinkled face. I want to laugh out loud. I am a pilgrim seeking absolution from your hands. My eyes start to blur.

'Are you there?'

Yes, I am still here.

'Yes, I'm here'.

'It's me, Arthur. I wanted to talk to you; I want to talk to you'.

'Shantih, shantih, shantih'.

-Upanishads

'What, then, is to be done? To make the best of what is in our power, and take the rest as it naturally happens'.

-Epictetus, Discourses

'Do not go gentle into that good night,
Old age should burn and rave at close of day;
Rage, rage against the dying of the light.'

-Dylan Thomas

'All that we are is the result of what we have thought: it is founded on our thoughts and made up of our thoughts.'

-Gautama Buddha, The Dhammapada

About the Author

Andy Owen served in the Intelligence Corps of the British Army reaching the rank of Captain. He completed operational tours in Northern Ireland (2003), Iraq (Baghdad 2004, Basra 2005) and on specialist intelligence duties in Helmand Province, Afghanistan in 2007. East of Coker is his second novel following Invective (2014). He now lives in London, UK.

Mission
To promote social change surrounding veterans issues through written awareness.

Vision
The War Writers' Campaign aims to maintain a long-term and historic platform that facilitates the consolidated efforts of service members and veterans to promote mental therapy through the literary word. Its continued purpose of affecting advocacy and assistance will shape and direct the programs of best in class veterans organizations for years to come.

The War Writers' Campaign, Inc. helps veterans in the following ways:

Assist veterans in telling their own story

Engage them where they are in the power of therapy through communication

Empower the next greatest generation of veterans through written publications that generate royalties, create awareness for change, and provide a platform for altruistic giving in the veteran space

Cultivate impact for tangible advocacy – 100% of proceeds from published works go directly back to best in class veterans programs

IRAQ AND AFGHANISTAN
VETERANS OF AMERICA

The War Writers' Campaign is proud to partner with Iraq and Afghanistan Veterans of America (IAVA).

Through our partnership, The Campaign is not only able to support the historical platform for veteran story; we are supporting best-in-class programs that improve the lives of veterans, their families, and our community. The War Writers' Campaign is able to bring together the voices of our Nation's heroes and leverage them for advocacy in the veteran space.

100% of all proceeds support the combined partnership programs of The Campaign and IAVA.

Iraq and Afghanistan Veterans of America (IAVA) is the first and largest nonprofit, nonpartisan organization for new veterans, with over 200,000 Member Veterans and supporters nationwide. IAVA is a 21st Century veterans' organization dedicated to standing with the 2.4 million veterans of Iraq and Afghanistan from their first day home through the rest of their lives.

Founded in 2004 by an Iraq veteran, their mission is to improve the lives of Iraq and Afghanistan veterans and their families. IAVA strives to build an empowered generation of veterans who provide sustainable leadership for our country and their local communities. They work toward this vision through programs in four key impact areas: supporting new veterans in Health, Education, Employment and building a lasting Community for vets and their families (HEEC).

IAVA creates impact in these critical areas through assistance to vets and their families, raising awareness about issues facing our community and advocating for supportive policy from the federal to the local level.

Learn more about IAVA by visiting their website: IAVA.org

All views expressed by authors of The War Writers' Campaign, Inc. are their own. The Iraq and Afghanistan Veterans of America (IAVA) partnership is not an endorsement of content, but for the platform of awareness itself and for the purposes of promoting funds to veteran causes.

CPSIA information can be obtained
at www.ICGtesting.com
Printed in the USA
LVOW12s1630121216
516922LV00006B/1434/P